Ex umbris et magnibus veritatem
Out of the shadows and images, into the Truth
John Cardinal Newman's epitaph

IN MEMORY OF MY PARENTS

Notes and Acknowledgements

Times and attitudes change. I have tried to re-create the mood of Victorian England as well as the attitude of its people to Roman Catholicism. Reading about Blessed Cardinal Newman helped me to understand the feelings prevalent during that era. *The Cameo* is not meant to reflect on the relationship between Protestants and Catholics today, which is quite different than it was in the 19th century. One thing that has radically changed is that those men who are ordained in the Church of England and then come into full communion with the Roman Church can still serve as Priests, even those who are married. No criticism of any Christian denomination is intended, but I have attempted to portray the struggle that a person might have in confronting misconceptions rampant at that time.

All the characters in *The Cameo* are fictional and are not based on any actual persons and any similarity is coincidental. Blessed John Newman is mentioned but does not appear in the narrative. I chose the surname *Bartoli* for one of the characters as my mother's maiden name was *Bartole* and I changed it into the Italian version.

The Bava-Baccaris Massacre, on May 7, 1898, is a true historical incident. The date and details about the assassination of King Umberto of Italy are also factual.

Horrors of the prison camps on the Thai and Burma border during the Second World War have been well-documented, and scores of men from the Allied side, as well as Asian laborers, died in these camps. Museums dedicated to their memory can be visited at Kanchanaburi, Thailand, a short distance from Bangkok.

Many people have helped me in the journey of this book. Firstly, I would like to thank Jim Mahony for the idea for the story: a legal dispute years ago in England which arose over the ownership of a brooch found in a house.

Several friends read the first drafts and gave their comments and criticisms. Isabel Didricksen spent many hours proofreading, and suggesting changes. Sister Bernadette Ward, *fmm* graciously took time from her busy schedule to read the manuscript and correct some of my errors. Florence Farrell gave me helpful ideas about the Victorian era and pointed out some inconsistencies in the story. Diane Jones and other authors on authonomy.com commented on England shortly after WWII. I would also like to thank Father David Bellusci for his contributions in the Italian letter in Chapter 13. Lastly, my good friend, Marlene Abbott, offered some much-needed encouragement. To all these friends, my heartfelt gratitude.

In researching the life of Cardinal Newman, I consulted the excellent biography by Ian Ker; *John Henry Newman: A Biography* (Oxford: Oxford University Press. 1988).

For information about the camps whose prisoners built the Thai-Burmese Railway, I am indebted to the book,

The Thai-Burma Railway, The True Story of the Bridge on the River Kwai. Bangkok, Thailand: Image Makers Co. Ltd. 2005.

The Force of Destiny by C. Duggan (London: Allen Lane, 2007) was my major source for the history of Italy.

Finally, I thank the editors and staff at CreateSpace for their help with the technical details of publishing.

Lorraine Shelstad
Maple Ridge, BC, Canada,
December, 2010

Chapter 1

As his mother followed James up the wide staircase she called out, "This is really lovely, James. It will suit you just fine." Markham House was a perfect home for him even though he would have been happier with a smaller place. James decided he liked the solid look of grey stone and the impressive bay window. And the more he thought about it, the more he looked forward to sitting in the oak-paneled library with a roaring fire, reading his books once again. Yes, this was the place he needed now that he had returned to England. It was far enough from London that he would have an excuse not to attend tiresome events; yet it was close enough to visit his parents when necessary.

His mother went on to investigate the next room, while James stood by the window and admired the view; an expanse of green lawn encircled by mature oak trees. It had been described in the brochure as "a perfect place for children to play". Not that he had any children yet and, heaven knows, if he ever would have. Sometimes he wished he were already married to some attractive, charming woman, settled down with a family. At other times he was glad he had no responsibilities and could enjoy his new-found freedom. He couldn't think of marriage right now in any case. First of all, he had to regain his health. Besides, this bloody war had changed so many things, most of all, his outlook on everything. Would anyone ever understand that?

His younger sister, Sarah, burst into the room interrupting his thoughts.

"It's a wonderful place. Elizabeth will love it." She left as quickly as she had come hurrying to see the other rooms.

Yes, Elizabeth ... everyone thought that she was the beautiful, charming woman destined to be his wife. Perhaps she was ... someday. He'd had girlfriends before the war, of course, some of them fairly serious at the time. There had been one in particular he thought he'd been in love with, but the feelings didn't last long and were based more on physical attraction than anything else. Elizabeth had always been there in the background, too; the daughter of his mother's best friend.

The next day Captain James Marsh went to the office of Winston Estates Ltd. and signed the lease. He moved his things and began to get settled into life in England. It was 1946 and the country was trying to get back to normal now that the war was over. There were still plenty of problems: rationing, unemployment, not to mention the rubble, left by bombing, to be cleared away. It would likely take many years before all these things were dealt with, but at least there wasn't the whine of sirens announcing approaching bombers. Nor did people dread a knock on the door, fearing news of a son or husband killed in action. *A noble death, but just as dead,* James thought rather grimly.

That spring the weather was cool, and life was somewhat ordinary after Asia. Thank God for that! It would take him a while to adjust to a normal life after what he had been through. Those few months in Singapore had already done wonders to restore his health. He'd put on some weight, in fact, although he was still thinner than usual, he almost looked like his former self. He had always been on the slim side and in those days he could even have been described as "tall, dark and handsome"!

And yes, Elizabeth did love the house when she came to see it. Possibly she, too, thought she was destined to be the lady of Markham House someday. After all, she and James had known each other since they were children.

As Markham House had been vacant for a while, one thing he had to do was to see that it was cleaned from top to bottom. He asked the housekeeper, Mrs. Lutton, a capable older woman who was in charge of the small number of staff, to do a thorough cleaning. He also had to attend to a few minor repairs, and the garden was a hopeless tangle of weeds. That would need looking after soon. If only he could find a decent gardener. All this kept his mind off the past, and that was the best thing for him now.

Work was started, and several days later, Mrs. Lutton knocked on the library door saying she wished to speak to the Captain if he were free.

"Certainly, come in."

"Sorry to bother you, sir, but I have something interesting to show you. One of the girls was dusting in the front bedroom and found this hidden in a crevice above one of the windowsills."

She held out her hand and in it he saw a brooch; a cameo with the Virgin Mary carved onto a pale creamy-pink background.

"It was very dusty but I cleaned it up and ... it's very beautiful, isn't it, sir? It doesn't look quite ... English somehow, with the Virgin Mary on it, you know. Who would have had it here, I wonder? Maybe they were hiding it and it slipped into the crevice," she shook her head in disbelief.

"Yes. It is a strange place to find a brooch. Thank you, Mrs. Lutton. I'll certainly look into it."

He ignored the comment about it not looking "English" for it definitely did look Roman Catholic. It seems that word was not out yet that the new occupant was both Roman Catholic *and* English.

He glanced at the brooch again; very delicate with a fine gold setting, put it in the top drawer of his desk, locked the drawer and then promptly forgot about it.

A week to the day James' memory was jogged when his phone rang. It was Mr. Winston.

"Hello, Captain Marsh? Henry Winston here. How are you enjoying your new home?"

"I'm enjoying it very much, thank you," James replied wondering what Mr. Winston was calling about.

"I was told that a valuable brooch was found in the house."

"Ye...s," James answered with caution, "There was a brooch found, but I haven't looked into its value yet. How did you find out about it?" He realized this would sound as if he had kept the brooch a secret and added, "Actually, I put it in a drawer and completely forgot about it until you called."

"Oh, you know, news of this nature, regarding valuable objects, does seem to travel rather quickly. I was wondering if you would be free to come round to my office this week to talk about it. Say Wednesday around two?"

"Yes, I could do."

"I'll see you Wednesday then? Oh, and could you bring the brooch with you?"

"Yes, of course."

Old Winston. Thinks he's being cheated out of a few pounds! James hung up the phone and unlocked the drawer to look at the cameo brooch again.

Wednesday, after an early lunch, James set out for the house of a Mr. Carelli. A friend had recommended him as an expert in antique jewelry. "He's Italian ... but they ended up on our side, after all," his friend said unnecessarily.

The red brick house was small, set beside similar houses. James knocked on the door and an older man answered.

"I've come to see Mr. Carelli. Is he in?"

The old man smiled broadly and looked up over his round, silver-rimmed glasses.

"Come in, come in. I'm sorry ... I used to have a shop before the war, but now...," he shrugged his shoulders, looked up to heaven and gave a sigh of resignation, "What can I do for you? I'm Mr. Carelli."

"I called earlier about a cameo brooch. I'm hoping you can tell me something about it, for example, if it is authentic and how much it is worth. A rough estimate will do."

James followed Mr. Carelli into the small sitting room and handed the brooch to him. The older man examined it closely and then held it up to the light of the window. He took a jeweler's magnifying glass, a loupe, from a drawer and looked at it more carefully.

"Do you wish to sell it?"

"It's not yet mine to sell," James answered, not going into detail.

"It's a good piece of carving; certainly authentic," Signore Carelli squinted as he looked up, "That is, it has been carved from carnelian shell in one piece, not attached after. This type of cameo is called "angelskin" because of the delicate pink color. You can see here ... it's signed by the artist on the back, *Il Greco*. He may have been Greek, but more likely that was his nickname. I'd guess from *Torre del Greco*, a town near Naples. It's famous for cameos. The cameo isn't old though ... only about 60 years."

"Then it's not worth much?"

"How a cameo is carved, and the subject, makes it rare and more valuable. There are many cameos from old Roman times; they may be older but not worth as much. Most are of classical scenes ... scenes with Greek or Roman gods and goddesses. Later ones are of women, usually profiles. The Virgin Mary was not carved often on cameos. That is strange, no? For there are many paintings of her. Why? I'm not sure."

"What would you estimate its value to be?"

"Because the subject is not that common, about £80 to a £100. The setting is eighteen carat gold, so it is very good."

"Thank you, Mr. Carelli. You've been very helpful," James said as he left a few shillings on a small table near the door.

James walked to Mr. Winston's office as it was not far. It was a clear sunny day; a day more for going for a ride in the country than for a meeting in a dingy office.

He entered the old brick building just off the High Street and was shown into an inner office by Winston's secretary, a middle-aged lady with dark blonde hair pulled back into a severe bun. He wondered why she never seemed to smile. Winston, with his usual florid complexion, was sitting at the head of a long, polished, wooden table. He was somewhat overweight, and this caused him to breathe with difficulty.

"Captain Marsh. Come in, come in. Do sit down." Oh yes, Mr. Winston was all charm and friendliness even though he had called him over to claim something that didn't belong to him. Winston's lawyer, George Spence, a middle-aged man, also with a portly figure, had already arrived and was sitting next to Winston. *He must think the brooch is worth a fortune,* James thought. Another older, thin gentleman sat beside at the far end of the table.

"I think you and Mr. Spence have already met. And this is Mr. Brigdon, who is an expert in cameos. Did you bring the brooch in question, Captain Marsh?" Mr. Winston peered at him with pale, watery blue eyes.

"Yes, I did. But shouldn't we discuss ownership of the brooch?"

"But surely you agree that you are leasing only the house with its furniture, therefore anything else found there would belong to me, the owner," Mr. Winston smiled easily.

"I believe that the law says that a lost article found by someone can only be kept by that person if he has taken reasonable steps to find the owner," James said as he handed the cameo over to Mr. Winston who glanced at it briefly and gave it to Mr. Brigdon. James had studied some Law while preparing for his military career and although he was not really interested in the cameo, he didn't want to make it too easy for Winston to claim it.

"Quite right, quite right," Mr. Winston said and turned to the thin man, "What do you think of the quality of the cameo, Brigdon?"

Mr. Brigdon took out a small magnifying glass, as Mr. Carelli had done, and proceeded to examine the brooch.

"It certainly looks authentic. Very likely from Italy. The subject, the Madonna, is not a particularly common one, at least in the better cameos, strange to say." It seemed Mr. Carelli and Mr. Brigdon certainly agreed on that.

"Does that make it more valuable?" Mr. Winston asked, rather anxiously.

"Oh, yes I would say so. Perhaps about £100. I wouldn't say more than a £100 though."

Mr. Winston raised his eyebrows. Was he expecting more or less? James could not tell for sure. It may be that £100 is not much to someone who already owns and leases out several large estates but, still, it was considerable.

"What does the law say about this kind of thing, Spence? Is Captain Marsh right?" Mr. Winston turned to his lawyer.

"Well, I think a court may rule on your behalf. After all, the brooch was found on your property even though you were not the finder. But ... it is true that a person who finds something which is not his must take "reasonable steps" to discover the owner of such property as Captain Marsh has said."

"I see." Mr. Winston was definitely deflated.

"I'd like to make a suggestion," James turned to Mr. Winston, "Rather than argue about the present ownership, I suggest we try to take those "reasonable steps" to find the original owner. I wouldn't mind volunteering my time to find that person. It could turn out to be interesting."

Mr. Winston pursed his lips. To be sure, this was not only the right thing to do but also he may be legally bound to do so. He was not always fair in his dealings, nor did he always follow the law strictly, especially when there was money involved. However, if he disagreed it would make him look mean-spirited and greedy, and this he could not afford to do. Also there was the vague chance that someone would find out about the cameo after and then claim it. Would he then face more problems; even more than the brooch was worth?

"A good idea, but couldn't someone falsely claim ownership? How would you know the person was truly the owner?"

"Well, they would have to describe the cameo; we've heard the Virgin Mary is an unusual subject."

"But there are those who work for you ... the women who found the cameo, for example. They could tell anyone what it looked like."

"Hmm ... that's true. We would have to require some proof. A receipt of purchase or even a photo of someone wearing the brooch would prove they were the owners."

Mr. Winston looked at Mr. Spence, "What do you think, Spence?" He thought the chance of someone having such proof was rather small.

"I think Captain Marsh has made an excellent suggestion. Anyone claiming to be the owner would have to have proof of ownership. If they don't have any evidence, then it would revert to you, Winston. Are you saying that you would be willing to look for the owner yourself, Captain Marsh?"

James smiled, "Well, I have been relieved of my duties temporarily in order to rest and get back into English society, but I dislike sitting around doing nothing. So, yes, I could do this."

"Well, that is good of you. Will you contact me when you have discovered something? And ... if you don't find anyone ... should we say, four months, for a time limit? That would make it the end of August."

"Yes, agreed." James rose to leave.

As he left he thought, *Good heavens, what have I let myself into?*

Chapter 2

The following day James contacted the Town Hall which had records of previous owners and tenants of Markham House. He made a list of the names, but thought it would not be wise to contact each one just now. Then he put a small ad in the local paper saying a brooch had been found at Markham House. He gave his name and address, asking anyone who knew anything about a lost brooch to contact him. He added that anyone who thinks the brooch is his should be able to give a description of it for identification. As well, the person should provide some proof of ownership, such as a bill of sale or a photo. He did not mention that the brooch was a cameo.

For a few days, James was busy with household accounts, contacting old friends in the area as well as getting in touch with several men in his regiment who lived in the area. His mother and his sister came to give their ideas about new decor and his mother thought he should give a party for their friends to see Markham House. He managed to postpone both the decorating and the party as he just didn't feel up to seeing a lot of people yet. He was certainly in no hurry to change anything in Markham House either. He rather liked it just the way it was.

Several days later he received a letter from a Mr. and Mrs. Cooper saying they had a brooch that was now missing. It was, they claimed, a cameo with a silhouette of a young girl with long, flowing hair. He called the number given and said that their description was not the same as the brooch in question. Then they altered their description slightly, saying that the girl's hair was done up and was not long and flowing. It had been a while since they had lost the brooch and they couldn't remember exactly what the girl's hair was like. He checked the list to see if anyone with the name "Cooper"' had ever lived at Markham House; there was no such name. It seemed likely that they were hoping to gain a brooch that was not theirs.

Later in the week, another person called, saying they lost a brooch while walking in the woods near Markham House. The brooch they had lost was a small gold brooch with several topaz stones set in it. James told them that, unfortunately, the brooch found at Markham House did not match their description.

The following week he received a note:

Dear Captain Marsh;

My family lived at Markham House about 40 years ago. I was only 10 years old and I remember my mother telling us a woman had written to her saying she was the daughter of the previous owner. It seemed that before she married and moved, she had a cameo brooch which she had misplaced at Markham House. She could not find the brooch and asked if we could look to see if it was still somewhere in the house. As sort of a game, my mother had my sister and I look for the brooch. We did not find anything, and my mother wrote back to tell the woman we hadn't found it. As I was fairly young at the time, I don't remember the woman's name or where she lived (somewhere near Oxford comes to mind, but I can't be certain). I hope this will somehow aid you in finding the owner.

Yours truly,
Mary Treleven.

James wrote a brief note to thank her for her help.

Almost a month after he put the advert in, James received another letter, this time more promising.

Dear Captain Marsh;

Regarding the item you placed in the paper last month, I may have some information for you concerning the brooch. My grandmother, whose maiden name was Ashford, lived at Markham House about fifty years ago. She had been given a cameo brooch with the Madonna in a gold setting when she was visiting Italy as a young woman in 1898.

She moved from Markham House when she married my grandfather. I had forgotten about the cameo brooch until I saw your advert and think that the brooch you have may be the one belonging to my grandmother who has since passed away.

I live at Littlemore, Oxfordshire and can be reached at the address above or after 5 pm by calling Oxford 9425 if you think that the brooch I described is the one in your possession.

Yours truly,
Claire Bromley

This time there was a good chance this person was the owner or at least the granddaughter of the owner. She had described the rare subject of the cameo, and her family had once lived at Markham House. He checked the list of previous owners and indeed "Ashford" was listed. But why had the cameo been forgotten until now? More importantly, would they have any proof of ownership? He decided to visit Miss Bromley. He called first to set up a time, and it was decided he would come the following Tuesday around 3 pm.

It was another warm summer day, perfect for the short drive to meet with the possible owner of the cameo. Elizabeth and Sarah had suggested earlier that they go on a picnic, but he had managed to get out of going without telling of his plans for the day. Somehow he didn't want to share this business of the cameo with anyone right now as it seemed a rather silly thing to be occupying the time of an army Captain. In any case, there was a likelihood he had found the owner in less than four months, the time stipulated by Mr. Winston. He would be surprised and probably disappointed, too.

James parked his old red MG in front of a plain, two-story brownstone house with a few early flowers in the tiny garden. He checked the address. Yes, this seemed to be the place. Odd that someone whose grandmother had once lived in Markham House lived in this rather unpretentious place.

He rang the bell, and a young woman with dark shoulder-length hair answered the door. She was dressed in a brown tweed skirt and pale green jumper, was of medium height and slim, with a good figure, he noted.

"Captain Marsh? I'm Claire Bromley. Please, do come in."

She showed him into a small but cozy room where a tiny, older lady was buried in a huge chair.

"Aunt Isabel, this is Captain Marsh from Markham House," her voice became louder as she spoke, "He has a cameo that may have been Grandmother's on Mother's side. Captain Marsh, my aunt, Mrs. Isabel Bromley."

Aunt Isabel acknowledged the visitor with a nod of her head and said something so softly he didn't hear.

Miss Bromley turned to James, "Please sit down, Captain Marsh. We were just about to have a cup of tea. Can I get you one?"

"Yes, I'd like that," James said as he sat down. The room was furnished in typical English middle-class style. There was a fireplace at one end, an over-stuffed brown sofa that matched the chair where Aunt Isabel sat, and a maroon, patterned rug on a polished hardwood floor. A wireless stood on one side of the room and next to it a small bookcase with a few small ornaments on top.

Miss Bromley brought three china cups, a teapot and some homemade biscuits on a tray. He first thought Claire Bromley plain but noticed that when she smiled she was really quite attractive.

James thought it was best to come to the point and explain about the cameo.

"Have you ever lived at Markham House, Miss Bromley?"

"Oh, good heavens, no. It was my grandmother's family's home. Her name was Claire Ashford ... I am named after her. When she married, she and my grandfather moved away to a cottage on the other side Oxford, where my mother still lives. I think her family lost Markham House when my great-grandfather died, I'm not sure why, but it may have been because of a bank failure. I'm staying with my aunt here in Littlemore as it's easier for me to get to work at the military hospital nearby. As a matter of fact, I've never even been to Markham House." She paused as she poured tea, "Have you lived there long?"

"I only moved in a month ago. I've been in Singapore since the war ended and returned recently. My parents have a house in London, but I preferred to live in the country."

"You must have found Singapore interesting. You weren't there during the war were you? They had a terrible time of it, from what I've heard."

"No, I wasn't. It's a fascinating place, but a lot of changes are in store ... independence and all."

"So I've heard. We have a lot of returned soldiers recuperating at the hospital, so I'm in touch with it a bit."

"Really? How interesting." Every time Miss Bromley smiled, James was struck with how pretty she was.

"Well, about the cameo," he abruptly changed the subject, "It was found by my cleaning staff in a crevice on top of a window ledge."

Miss Bromley laughed, "How very odd."

"Yes, quite. The owner of Markham House claims that legally the brooch belongs to him, but I suggested we try to find the actual owner which is why I put an ad in the paper," he explained, "You've correctly identified the subject of the cameo, but I'm afraid you'll need some proof that it belonged to your Grandmother in order for you to claim it. A photo or ... something like that."

"Yes, you mentioned that in your ad and I've been thinking about what we have. We don't have a photo of my grandmother wearing it, but we do have a diary that she kept while she was in Italy. I once read her account of being given the cameo. Would that do? I brought the diary back when I visited my mother last weekend but I haven't mentioned anything about the brooch to her yet. I don't want to disappoint her if it turns out not to be Grandmother's."

She got up, picked up a small, brown, leather-covered book from a table nearby and handed it to him.

"You're welcome to take it with you. You may find it boring to read all the way through, though I found it interesting. I suppose because it's my grandmother's story. Here, I marked the page where she tells about the brooch if you just want to read that."

"Thank you. I'll eventually have to take the diary to show to Mr. Winston. Unfortunately, he locked the cameo in his safe, so I can't show it to you."

"I was hoping to see it. Is it worth a lot of money then?" she asked with genuine surprise in her voice.

"It's been valued at about £80 to £100. A reasonable sum," he explained.

"I'm surprised. After all, it couldn't be all that old. Cameos from Victorian times are fairly common, I expect."

"I understand it's the subject, for one thing, the Virgin Mary, which makes it a bit rare but you're right, it's not that old ... around the early 19th century."

"You seem to know a lot about cameos." That smile again.

"I was told this when I took the brooch to a jeweler to have it valued. Believe me, I knew nothing about cameos before."

They chatted for a while about her work at the hospital, and he was able to avoid talking about Singapore. Aunt Isabel had dozed off in her chair after finishing her tea.

"Well, I'd better be going. Please say "Good-by" to your Aunt from me. Good Lord, it's almost 5! I hope I haven't kept you from something. I'd no idea it was so late."

"Oh no, just housework! I'm always glad to have an excuse not to do that."

"I'll take the diary then, if you trust me with it, and I'll contact you in a week or so about the decision. Hopefully Mr. Winston will agree you are the rightful owner. Is there anyone else that could claim it?"

"My grandmother only had one daughter ... my mother. She is the rightful heir, if it is my grandmother's cameo. I had a brother, but he was killed in the war. In France." A shadow of pain briefly crossed her face. The war had changed everyone's life, not just his.

"I'm sorry. I hope after what the world has just been through we've seen the last of war."

"Well, the first World War was supposed to end all wars, wasn't it? We didn't seem to learn any lessons then."

"We didn't have much choice about fighting this time. Well, I hope to get in touch with you soon," he smiled and turned towards his car. "I was wondering if you'd like to visit Markham House·sometime and see your Grandmother's former home."

"That would be lovely." She waited until his car turned at the corner and then went inside.

Had it been cowardly of him or just plain deceitful to say he hadn't been in Singapore during the war? Well, it was the truth, in a way. He hadn't been there long before the Japanese had surprised everyone and attacked Singapore from Malaya instead of from the sea. After a short time in Changi prison, they'd marched him with the others up to the Siam-Burmese border where they'd spent the rest of the war hacking out jungle for a railroad. So it was true, he hadn't actually been in Singapore during the war. He hated to mention it or even think about that time. People always tried to make appropriate comments, "How awful it must have been." or "How dreadful for you." But there was nothing they could say that would have been adequate. No comment that could wipe out the disease and the stench, of watching your own soldiers and others slowly die. He did not understand how he had survived it. How had anyone survived it?

This was the real reason he could not live in London and attend his mother's parties or meet his father's acquaintances. He didn't seem to have anything in common with his old friends, Elizabeth or even his own family. How could they understand that his outlook on life had been changed forever?

No, it was best to live in the country and try to keep occupied with other things. Ordinary things, so he could gradually adjust back to life in Britain. Even things like an old cameo brooch.

Chapter 3

When James had finished dinner that evening, he poured a brandy, sat in the most comfortable chair in the library, and started reading the diary. As he read, he unconsciously pictured the writer as her namesake, Claire Bromley.

∽

Tuesday, March 8, 1898.

Dear Diary;

I should be excited, but I'm not. Father is sending me to the Continent because of my health. Mother gave me you, my new diary, so that I can write about my trip and the thoughts I will have as I travel. My mother's friend, Dorothea Weston, will be going as my chaperone, because she has been to Italy before. She seems a bit strict, but I hope I'm wrong about her. I hope that she'll turn out to be an agreeable companion.

Mother and Father are worried about me because I haven't been well lately. The weather this winter has been unusually rainy and dull and they blame it on that. Because Italy is warmer and sunnier, they hope my health will improve. I am not sure.

Weather is certainly part of the problem ... but not all. My feeling unwell began when my younger cousin, Elsa, became engaged to Andrew Holton in April. It's not exactly that I am in love with him, but he has been a friend for a long time, and I always thought that he would marry me; certainly not Elsa. They seem completely unsuited to each other. Andrew is tall, fair and very handsome (at least I think he is), and he truly did seem to like me in a special way. I think we have a lot in common. We both like walking in the country and reading poetry, but don't like parties. Elsa, on the other hand, loves parties and people call her a "social butterfly". Elsa flirted and giggled until Andrew turned his attentions towards her. I think flirting gives a false impression somehow ... why do women have to resort to it? Surely our intelligence should serve instead to attract a man of real character? In any case, I am determined never resort to it!

When you reach my age, one begins to worry about whom one will marry. After all, I'm already eighteen! It isn't that I want to get married immediately, for then I will have many responsibilities, and I'm not ready for those yet. On the other hand, someday I do want to marry, and most of us hope to marry someone they love or at least feel some affection for. But things are not that certain, and I fear that I will either not fall in love or will have to marry someone I do not love. Those possibilities always loom before me. The alternative would be never to marry, which would be worse. An unmarried woman is simply not accepted in polite society.

Usually, it is the eldest son in the family who inherits the family home, as well as money. Since there aren't many things a woman can do to support herself nowadays, what does one do? Even being a governess has gone out of fashion. I'm sure that my brother, George, would see I was provided for but still ... that may not always be possible. I suppose

Dorothea is my travelling companion just because of this ... she has never married.

When I did feel unwell it just didn't seem worthwhile getting over. I am always tired and don't feel like doing anything. Dr. Church does not think I have consumption, which sounds romantic in novels but would not be that romantic in reality. Someday I may meet a dull, ordinary-looking man who will marry me, but right now even that doesn't look promising. Of course, my parents know nothing of my feelings.

It is still cold and dreary; the weather this spring hasn't improved much. Sometimes, when I'm sitting in my room, it feels as if my blood has turned to ice.

Yesterday, Elsa came to tell us about her new gowns and plans for her wedding. Andrew also came. It was difficult to act pleasant seeing them steal glances at each other, not sharing their secrets with me. As childhood companions, the three of us shared absolutely everything!

You can see why I am not too excited to be going to Italy. Yet it will be better to be somewhere else where I will have other things to occupy my mind. I will be able to escape from this dreary landscape and see new places I have only dreamed about up until now. We will be going to a place in Tuscany in Italy, since Dorothea has been there before with her parents. She says it is "a safe, quiet place" but not so "safe or quiet" that it is not interesting, I hope. We'll go first to Florence in order to see the magnificent art of the Renaissance. The best news is that we will be away until after Easter and not come back to England until it is warmer. I must go now as I have a lot to do in preparation for our trip.

It is Wednesday, and it seems I have been sorting and packing for ages. It's very difficult to decide what to take. At least it gives me something to keep my mind off our trip itself and leaving home, which is a good thing. I have had some new dresses made for Italy's warmer climate, and

I am excited about that. Already I feel better because I have something to look forward to. I have mixed emotions ... I look forward to the excitement of traveling, but I dread leaving my family.

We leave tomorrow which may cause me to miss several days of writing. First, we will cross the channel to France and then go by ship from the south of France to Leghorn, on Italy's western coast. Only Nora is going with us, so she will be very busy attending both Dorothea and myself.

Dorothea arrived yesterday morning. My parents have asked her every possible question about where we are going, and they have told her all their expectations and rules. Furthermore, they are constantly reminding me how I should act, what I should wear, what I should do, and most of all, what I should not do.

Thursday, March 10. We said our "Good-byes", and, as expected, we shed a few tears, or at least, I did. I realize that this is the first time I will be away from home for such a long time. The thought of that is frightening in some ways. What if I am unhappy there? What if I miss my family so much that I become homesick? I won't be able to return earlier than planned as we cannot change our passage easily. I am a little nervous and apprehensive about it all. My younger sisters, Beth and Margaret, wished they were going instead but, if they were going, I'm certain they would feel as I do. George came from Oxford to see me before I leave. How good it was to see him again! Unfortunately, we didn't have much of a chance to visit.

My entire family went to the docks to see us off, and it was mayhem there. So many people seeing their families and friends off to faraway, romantic places! We had to arrange to have our trunks put on board and, then, board ourselves. Boarding the large ferry, the noise of the people and the loud horn made me more apprehensive, but it was also very exciting. As we pulled away from the dock, I could see my parents, my sisters, my brother, and Elsa and Andrew waving to us. I waved back and watched them get smaller and smaller, until finally, I could not see them any longer.

The crossing of the English Channel was rough, and I was thankful when we reached Calais safely. I had not been able to eat a thing the entire trip, so I was famished when we arrived in France. While we were on the ship it was grey and rainy, making it impossible to sit outside. I am hoping the trip improves from here on, or I shall certainly wish I had never left home.

It is already March the 15th, and I have missed writing for a few days. Our trip overland from Calais to Nice was extremely tiring, although there were many new experiences. It was the first time I had travelled on a train—a French train at that! It was fairly comfortable, and we had adequate meals but not as good as I expected French food to be. We passed by Paris. Although I would have loved to have seen "the City of Lights", Dorothea said it is just too crowded and expensive ... and too wicked! We arrived in Nice, a charming city with a view of the Mediterranean coastline. There are trees and flowers here that I have never seen before, and it has been sunny and warm the entire time. Yesterday we walked along the seaside; so many English come here the French call it *Promenade des Anglais* or "The English Walk". How crowded it is! All sorts of people (and not just English): people walking their funny little dogs, women showing off the newest fashions and couples in love, unaware of anyone else around them. I look at them, and wish that I had someone who loved me.

Yesterday, we boarded the packet ship which will take us to Italy. Dorothea and I each have comfortable rooms. Since we left Marseilles, I've not been sick even once and, for that, I am grateful. It seems that I will truly be able to enjoy our journey on the Mediterranean. Most days we have been able to sit outside where we enjoy the sunshine, although there is often a brisk breeze with a biting chill.

We have met a few other English who are travelling to Italy. There are also a some French on board; most are business men travelling to Milan, I think. I met the daughter of one, Madeleine Dubois, who, thankfully, speaks a little English. She is petite, pretty and has exquisite clothes and I admit to a bit of jealousy. With my paltry French and her simple English, we do have some interesting conversations. We cannot talk about much, but we laugh at our attempts.

We docked in Leghorn or Livorno, in Italian. I said good-bye to Madeleine who is going on to Milan with her father. I do hope that I meet someone else along the way I can be friends with.

After many days traveling by ship, train and coach, we have finally reached Florence. We are staying at a small hotel near the Arno River where a few other English guests are staying. It seems it is still fashionable to travel to the Continent, especially to see the art of the Medieval and Renaissance periods. Everyone at this hotel is a self-proclaimed expert on some artist or period. To be truthful, I have become quite tired of hearing about Michelangelo, Fra Angelico, and Leonardo da Vinci!

Today we went to the *Cathedral of Santa Maria del Fiore,* which means the Cathedral of Mary of the Flowers. There is a bell tower, designed by Giotto, beside it. The dome of the cathedral is very large, and its construction marked the beginning of the Renaissance, so the experts here, armed with their Murray's Guides, say! Wherever one looks in Florence, you can see the huge, red dome presiding over its own city like a great dowager Queen.

We also saw the octagonal Baptistery of St. John with the famous bronze doors by Lorenzo Ghiberti. The south ones have scenes from the New Testament, whereas the east doors have scenes from the Old Testament. Michelangelo declared them fit to be the Gates of Paradise, which is why they are called this even today.

We visited the Pitti Palace, as well as the Uffizi Gallery; both have many paintings, mostly of the Virgin Mary and Jesus or other scenes from Scripture. Portraits of the Medici family and other famous Florentines of the 14th century are also amongst the collection. There must be hundreds of paintings of the Annunciation and even more of the Crucifixion! There are just too many for me to remember. I do like the rich colours the artists used: vivid blues, soft roses, pale greens. The way they used light to illuminate people's faces in their paintings is truly magnificent.

The highlight today, according to the "experts", was to see "David" in the *Galleria dell'Accademia* where the huge sculpture was moved about twenty years ago. This is Florence's most famous sculpture by Michelangelo. I suppose one must recognize it as the outstanding art it is, but I don't think we would ever have a sculpture of a naked man in England, even though we English may flock to Florence to see it. What hypocrites we sometimes are! Someone remarked that there is a copy of David in a gallery in London, but it has a fig leaf which can be added when women are present. Imagine!

We visited some other churches and museums with those from our hotel. I am looking forward to being outside more and enjoying nature. This is what I hope we can do when we finally get to the hill town of Montepulciano.

The food in Florence is delicious! I do not eat much at home, but here it is a different matter. I'm afraid that I will eat too much and not be able to wear my new dresses. We have something called *pasta* made with eggs and flour which is then formed into different shapes: spirals, little shells or tubes. This is served with a creamy sauce, and after, we are served meat or fish with vegetables. It all tastes different than food at home because of the herbs and seasonings they use. I am enjoying the Italian food now but after a few weeks, even I may long for some English roast beef.

It is strange to think that we are in a foreign country, hearing a language we cannot understand. England seems far away, and it feels that it is a long time ago that we left it. I have to pinch myself to see if I am truly here, and that this is not a dream. We have only been here a fortnight, and in a couple of days, we will be leaving for Montepulciano where we will stay until we return to England.

Today (Friday, March 18th), we joined a group from our hotel to visit *Casa Guidi*, where Robert Browning and Elizabeth Barret Browning lived for fifteen years. Apparently, all English tourists dutifully come here to see the house near the Pitti Palace where they lived. I remember studying Elizabeth Barret Browning's poem, *The Casa Guidi Windows*. It was one of my favourite poems, but I never thought that one day I would see the place where it was written.

For lunch, we had a Tuscan soup made of beans and bread. It was very different but surprisingly delicious. We were told that Tuscans are called *mangia faggioli* or "bean eaters" because they eat like to eat beans!

This afternoon Dorothea and I shopped for gifts to take back home. I bought my mother a pair of soft chamois leather gloves. They are the color of cream, and so exquisite I wish I had bought a pair for myself, as well. For my sisters, I bought two delicate gold chains from a shop on the *Ponte Vecchio*, which is famous for its many gold shops.

We leave early tomorrow for Montepulciano. I wonder what it will be like.

Chapter 4

As we approached Montepulciano, I knew that I would like it immensely. We could see it perched on its own hilltop; ochre-coloured buildings looking as if they could easily tumble down into the olive groves below. It must have appeared the same to knights returning home from the Crusades.

We are staying in a pleasant place, I think, although Dorothea says the carpets are a bit shabby and not too clean. The bed sheets, on the other hand, are whiter than I've ever seen and have the smell of fresh air. Unfortunately, we didn't have any marmalade for breakfast, much to Dorothea's dismay. I rather liked the plum preserve we had instead.

We are staying at a guesthouse, *Albergo Vittoria*, named after Queen Victoria, because it is owned by an Englishman. Mr. Balfour is a rather grey-looking man; tall and thin with grey hair, a grey face and sharp features. We only see his Italian wife, Maria, when she is serving us our meals or cleaning. She is a small, shy woman with thick, black hair done up in braids and an olive complexion. I think she would be more attractive if she wore her hair in a different fashion but I suppose she doesn't have time, as she is always rushing around cleaning or cooking. Maria Balfour speaks only a little English, so her husband deals with the hotel guests.

They have three children; a young, pretty girl who helps her mother (and is a younger version of her) and a boy about ten who goes off to school each morning and returns in the late afternoon. The youngest child, a darling little boy, is only about a year old. He is usually in the kitchen and, unfortunately, we rarely see him.

Our hotel is in one of the many narrow streets of the town. These streets wind around; meandering in a haphazard way. Some buildings are joined by graceful arches above the lanes, and you have to go down some crooked steps and under an archway to get to the street below.

Inside, *Albergo Vittoria* looks ancient, with wooden-beamed ceilings. There is an arched doorway leading to the dining room where we eat our meals at a long, polished wooden table. Across from the dining room is a sitting room with several old, comfortable sofas and a few chairs covered in flowered chintz. I like to imagine the people who lived here in the Middle Ages. Were they important and rich; artists or merchants who became rich by trading with the Byzantines?

My bedroom upstairs has a huge, iron bed with a headboard on which delicate flowers have been painted. On the opposite wall, there is a large armoire made of chestnut wood, a mirror, and a plain stand with a pitcher and washbasin. Above the bed, a wooden crucifix is hanging; not a plain cross as we would have in our homes, if we had one at all. Dorothea took hers down and put it in a drawer. She said, "The Lord has risen. He's not still on the cross." She promised to put it back when she leaves. I left mine up. Perhaps it is a good thing to be reminded of Jesus' suffering for us.

Since this hotel specializes in entertaining British travellers, there are four other British tourists here: Rev. Houghton, a Church of England clergyman from Oxford, who comes almost every year; Mr. and Mrs. Pierce from Birmingham and Miss Trent, Mrs. Pierce's niece, who is traveling with them. Rev. Houghton is tall and thin, with a rather gaunt look about him. His hair is greying at the temples, and his nose is rather large, but it is his smile that one notices first. It is the kind of smile that makes you feel he is genuinely interested in you. Mr. and Mrs. Pierce are well-matched; both look fairly ordinary, on the plump side with plump, jolly faces. They are almost always smiling which makes them appear most agreeable. Miss Trent, though, is petite and pretty and looks like a most interesting person. She wears her amber-coloured hair swept up in charming curls. Her teeth are ever so slightly crooked but rather than detracting from her beauty, this defect somehow adds to it. Her complexion is clear; her voice is pleasant. She appears to be a few years older than I am.

There are no guests my age yet, but Dorothea says some may come while we are still here. Everyone seems most amiable and I am looking forward to knowing them better. I hope that Miss Trent and I become good friends.

From my bedroom window, I can see the Chianti Valley. There are many shades of green, gold and brown and the fields are laid out in an intricate design reminding me of some mosaics we saw in Florence. Directly below me, I can see ancient, clay-tiled roofs and to the far left is a church (I can just see a huge dome) that rings its bells every morning and evening. I love the sound of the bells; joyful and mournful at the same time. How can that be? When I hear their regular, slow rhythm, I imagine people scurrying out of their houses down the hill to the church. But, since I cannot see the road at all from here, I may be quite wrong.

I could look out my window forever, especially when the sun is setting; the colour of the sky and the fields gradually fade, until finally, it is completely dark and I can just see black silhouettes of the houses and the church.

Today, as it is Sunday, we had Morning Prayers at the Guesthouse led excellently by Rev. Houghton. Later, in the afternoon, we went to see the town square or *Piazza Grande*. Miss Trent came with us. I think we will make a good threesome.

The cathedral has a rough, unfinished outside wall and faces the main square. After the many wonderful churches we saw in Florence, I am dismayed that this cathedral looks so unattractive. Besides the cathedral, there is a town hall, a tower and several cafés around the square.

It was pleasant sitting at one of the tables in the *piazza*. Large rectangles of light intersected the square, making everything appear golden and warm. I felt as if we were subjects in a Renaissance painting.

We were enjoying the view when a young man came up to our table. I was surprised that Dorothea knew him already. She introduced him to Miss Trent and me. It seems that yesterday Dorothea had arranged for me to have a tutor at my father's request. Apparently, he wants me to learn something while I am here!

"Signore Bartoli, this is your student, Miss Claire Ashford. And Miss Trent, who is also staying at the Guest House. Miss Trent, Claire; Signore Bartoli. Your father wanted me to engage a tutor so that you could learn about the history, language and art of Tuscany," Dorothea turned to me to explain, "We hope that Signore Bartoli will take us to see some sights of Tuscany and tell us the history of this area. Anyone at *Albergo Vittoria* is welcome to come with us, of course, especially you, Miss Trent. Mr. Bartoli will be our guide as well as your tutor, Claire."

"How do you do," was all I could manage to say. I was quite speechless, as until then I had never heard of such a plan. I should have thought either Father or Dorothea could have mentioned it to me beforehand, but as Signore Bartoli seemed fairly pleasant, I decided to forgive them. At least we will see some interesting sights and learn about them from a true native of Tuscany. Dorothea told me later that she had asked Mr. Balfour for help in finding someone. He suggested Mr. Bartoli who often comes to talk with Mr. Balfour in order to speak English.

Mr. Bartoli is slight in stature, has chestnut brown hair that is a little curly and wears round spectacles which give him a scholarly look. His complexion is fair, and his fine features make him look very young, I think.

"I am pleased to meet you. My name is Raffaele," Mr. Bartoli's accent was barely noticeable, "My parents named me after an angel thinking it would make me well-behaved, but, unfortunately, it did not help."

Raffaele. What a strange name. I have heard of the angels Michael and Gabriel, but I've never heard of any angels named Raffaele. Of course, I didn't admit it.

"There is one thing that you mentioned yesterday, Miss Weston," he turned to Dorothea, "It is a small problem. You said I was not to teach the Roman Catholic religion to Miss Ashford, but it is impossible to avoid when telling about our history or our art. Everything here in Toscana is associated with our Church," at this he made a sweeping motion with his arms, "It is a part of us."

"Oh, I understand. This was Claire's father's request, but I understand that you must include your religion when talking about art or telling us about the history of Tuscany. I have been here before, as you know. We do want to know about the Etruscans who were here before Christianity, too. Although we would like very much to see your churches and the art in them, we will not attend Mass as we will have our own services at the Guesthouse." Dorothea was of the evangelical wing of the Church of England and was very particular in her beliefs.

"I understand. Of course, there is no need to go to Mass."

"I think Mr. Ashford meant he did not want you to try to convert his daughter to Roman Catholicism," Dorothea added, unnecessarily. I doubt that my father had made that request; it would be quite out of character for him.

"Oh, of course not. I could never do that. That is up to God," the Angel answered good-naturedly and he looked up to heaven and then at me with a mischievous twinkle in his warm brown eyes.

It appeared that Dorothea completely missed the joke. She turned to me, "You would like to learn some Italian, too, wouldn't you Claire?"

"I suppose so, if that is what Father wished, but I'm afraid I am not particularly good at languages." I was trying hard to be serious and not giggle at Mr. Bartoli's comment.

"Well, I shall begin by getting you a cold drink, as the heat is unbearable today. I'll get some *limonate* ... you will already know what that means."

Mr. Bartoli went across the square to the café, and brought four large glasses of ice cold lemon cordial.

The remainder of the afternoon passed quickly. While Miss Trent and Dorothea talked, I was able to ask Signore Bartoli some questions. I learned that he is studying law at the University in Siena near here, but he has time to do some teaching. He spent a year in England which is when he learned English. He has one older brother who helps his father with their estate where they grow olives, and a younger sister who is still in school. I must say that I like Mr. Bartoli's way of speaking English; a slight prolonging of the vowels and consonants. It is not at all unpleasant.

And he told me that his name is written as *Raphael* in English and is the name of an angel in the book of Tobit. We do have this book in the English Church but we consider it an Apocryphal book, so we rarely read from it. I have heard of the artist Raphael; we saw some of his works while in Florence, so I should have recognized the name, I suppose.

Mr. Bartoli seems relaxed and entirely free of all falseness. He does not try to impress; although he was pleasant enough, I think that if people do not like him as he is, he does not try to be anything else. I wonder what kind of a tutor he will be. I thought tutors are all stern and strict but, Mr. Bartoli does seem to have a sense of humour, at least.

Mr. Bartoli explained that the outside of the cathedral or the *duomo* was never finished because the city ran out of money in the 16th century. This is why it looks rough on the outside wall and not at all attractive. He said it probably never will be completed, as now people are used to it and probably wouldn't like it any other way!

"Some day we will go inside to see the paintings and sculptures. The inside is much nicer," he promised.

He also told us that the building across from the *Duomo* is the *Palazzo Comunale* which is a copy of the *Palazzo Vecchio* that we saw in Florence. One of the other buildings, a palace called the *Palazzo Contucci,* belongs to a noble family. It does not look anything like a palace from outside, but we were told it is very splendid inside.

The three of us returned to the guesthouse in time for dinner, which was roast chicken. In Italy, the main meal of the day is eaten at noon and then the stores and offices close, so that people are able to rest during the hottest part of the day. I don't know if we will follow Italian or English custom at the Guesthouse, but today, at least, the main meal was in the evening.

Tonight I saw another magnificent sunset. The sky was the colour of the blood oranges we had at breakfast and the purple grapes we had at lunch. If it had not been a sunset, the colours would have been far too garish. Just before dark, a group of birds ... were they swallows? ... swooped over the fields. And the bells of the church clanged in the distance as they have for centuries, I suppose. Why do I feel I have been here before?

Monday. I dreamt about Andrew last night. He had decided not to marry Elsa after all and had come to Italy to find me. He bought me a *limonate,* and we sat in the piazza looking at the unfinished cathedral. It was a strange but happy dream ... Andrew was especially sweet and kind to me. When I woke up and realized it was a dream, I felt sad, and I really did not feel like going anywhere. However, there was no getting out of it, so I forced myself to get ready. More paintings in more churches, I supposed.

After eating breakfast, we sat in the sitting room waiting for Signore Bartoli, who was late. When he did come, he did not apologize but declared enthusiastically, "Today we have good weather. We will go for a walk to see the *Basilica of the Madonna of St. Bagio,* which is below the town. On our way back, we can see some other churches. In Italian, church is *chiesa.*"

"Is it always this pleasant in March?" Dorothea asked as we walked out to the street.

"Usually it doesn't get too hot until July or August. I hope we will have many more nice days while you are here," Signore Bartoli explained while we walked down a steep path leading from the street to a road below.

Like a true gentleman, Mr. Bartoli helped us when walking became difficult. Miss Trent came along, too. I have discovered her name is Celia. What a charming name! She seems shy by nature, but when she does say something it is intelligent. I would guess that she has a generous dose of English common-sense.

Soon we were below the town on a country road; the city wall and buildings with their roofs of terra-cotta tiles were above us on our left. On our right were rows of large, gnarled vines, with a few budding green leaves. I could smell the mouldy, earthy scent of spring.

"This is where we grow the *Sangiovese* grapes for our wine, *Vino Nobile di Montepulciano*. It is a red wine. Have you had any yet? We can taste some on our way back."

"I don't think we've had any at yet," Celia answered, "I think they serve a cheaper wine at the guesthouse." The meals are filling but a bit on the ordinary side, similar to what we would have in England. I suppose we are served English food (except marmalade) because most of the English guests wouldn't like anything too different from what they are used to eating.

Ahead of us we could see the huge Basilica with its turquoise dome. We passed a few farm houses and a cemetery with cypress trees like dark sentinels guarding the road leading to it. Then, suddenly in front of us was the church on an immense square of lawn that in spite of our decline was still high above the *Val di Chiana*. Gusts of wind whipped our skirts making it difficult to walk.

"This church was built in the 16th century; it is made of travertine marble in the shape of a Greek cross. *St. Bagio* ... I think he is St. Blaise in English ... is the Saint we ask to heal sore throats because he once healed a little boy who was choking on a fish bone," Mr. Bartoli pointed to his throat, "On his Feast Day in February, the priest blesses our throats."

Miss Trent commented that *San Bagio's* reminded her of St. Paul's in London, especially the dome.

We went inside, and there was no one else around. On entering the church, Mr. Bartoli, dipped his fingers in the holy water by the door, and made the sign of the cross. I wondered if I should do the same, but the others didn't, so I didn't either. Maybe it's not always best to "do in Rome as the Romans do".

From inside, the dome looked even larger than it had looked outside. Sunlight poured through a round opening at the top, and the dust in the air turned to swirling gold specks. The shaft of light reminded me of something. Then I remembered the paintings of The Annunciation we had seen in Florence with a ray of light piercing the clouds and touching the Virgin.

"It's very beautiful." I loved the echo of our voices and footsteps on the marble floor.

"Do you still use this church?" Dorothea asked.

"Yes, of course, there are many churches in Montepulciano and all of them have Masses several times a day. *San Bagio* has a Mass at 7:00 in the morning and again in the evening. You can hear its bells ringing every morning to announce Mass."

"Those are the bells I hear in each morning. I love that sound. It sounds so welcoming."

Dorothea looked at me, raising her eyebrows.

"It is not that welcoming if you still want to sleep," Signore Bartoli laughed.

On our way back, as promised, we stopped at a farm to taste some of their wine. Because we were now climbing up the hill, we were ready for a little rest. A huge man with black hair and a matching black moustache led us to a building behind the main house. The *cantina*, lined with large wooden barrels, was cool and musty smelling. Some very dusty, green bottles were stacked on the shelves at one end. Our host screwed a small tap into one of the barrels and served us each a glass of deep garnet-colored wine. He was constantly staring at me, and finally, he spoke to Mr. Bartoli. Mr. Bartoli leaned towards me, "He says your skin is *bella*. He would like to kiss you."

I was shocked and could feel my face become hot. Then Mr. Bartoli became embarrassed, too, and reassured me, "Don't worry, it's just his way of saying he thinks you are pretty. I told him that English ladies don't kiss strangers."

"And Italian ladies, do they kiss strangers?" Dorothea asked.

Mr. Bartoli shrugged his shoulders turning his palms up, "No, no. I'm sure they don't. I have never been kissed by one." He was, of course, teasing and lessening the tension.

I am not an expert on wine, therefore I don't know if it was a good wine or not. In any case, the visit had been spoiled for me.

We walked back into town. Since it was uphill going back, we were exhausted and very warm when we arrived at the top of the road. Mr. Bartoli was still enthusiastic and wanted to take us to other churches, but we begged to go back to *Albergo Vittoria* for a rest and leave them for another day.

Chapter 5

James had some business in London and thought it was a good opportunity to visit his parents while he was there.

When he returned to Markham House, he decided to call Claire Bromley and see if she were free to visit this week.

"Hello, Miss Bromley? This is James Marsh. I wonder if you are free this week to come and see your grandmother's former home."

"I am free this Saturday, as a matter of fact. Would that be convenient for you?"

"Yes, splendid. See you on Saturday then. I'll pick you up at your place about eleven, if that's alright. We can have lunch at Markham House."

"That would be fine."

Claire Bromley seemed to enjoy her visit to Markham House. It was interesting for her to see where her grandmother had grown up.

"I always imagined it like this," she admitted, "In which room did you find the brooch? That would have been my grandmother's room, I suppose." James showed her that room and the other rooms as well.

They had a light lunch of roast chicken and salad which had been prepared by the cook, and decided to eat it in the garden as it was a lovely, sunny day. It had been a long time since James had enjoyed an afternoon as much.

On the way back, they drove for a while in silence, enjoying the scenery.

"There is something I wasn't completely honest about the last time we spoke," James began. Claire turned to him with a questioning look.

"You asked if I was in Singapore during the war and I said, "No." In a way, that's true. But I *was* there when the Japanese invaded Singapore. We were thrown into Changi prison. A few months later, we were marched up through Malaya, north to Siam to build a supply railroad to Burma for the Japanese army."

"I've heard about those prison camps. Conditions there were pretty awful, weren't they?"

"That's an understatement. It was the closest thing to hell I can imagine."

"So much suffering all over the world," Claire said with a genuine sadness in her voice.

"The worst thing is when people say to me, "How brave you were." when you know damn well most of the time you were scared to death."

"Surely, it's not wrong to be frightened at such times," Claire answered in a quiet voice.

That evening as he sat in his usual chair and picked up the diary to read, he realized that Claire Bromley was not exactly the same as her grandmother.

༄

Tuesday, March 22, 1898

The weather has turned wet, cold and windy, so every-one thought it would be best not to go out today. Dorothea announced it was a perfect day to begin my Italian lessons. I suppose it will give me something to do when the weather is dull or we aren't going anywhere. Dorothea has said that she already knows enough Italian from the time she was here before; she can ask the necessary questions she needs to find her way around. Celia is not interested in learning Italian because she probably won't return. I am not sure why I am studying Italian, since I probably will never return to Italy either. But it is fashionable at home for young ladies to learn Italian, so I will try.

Celia and Dorothea talked with Rev. Houghton and the Pierces, who are also house-bound because of the rain. They found some puzzles in the Guesthouse's small library and worked on them. Then Celia played the piano and they all sang, providing entertainment for themselves. I must admit that Celia plays the piano very well.

Mr. Bartoli and I sat at a table at the far end of the sitting room where we could work without being disturbed. It seems that, although there are many dialects of Italian, the Italian in this part of Tuscany is considered to be the purest and most correct. I'm not certain how they decided this.

Mr. Bartoli began my lesson by teaching me greetings,

> *Buon giorno, signore* (Good day, sir)
> *Buona sera, signora* (Good evening, Madam) and
> *Arrivederci* (Goodbye)

Then I learned the verb "to be" which is *essere* and is conjugated as follows:

> *io sono* I am
> *tu sei* you are
> *lui or lei è* he or she is
> *noi siamo* we are
> *voi siete* you are
> *loro sono* they are

Now I can say, *Io sono Inglese* or "I am English".

Italian seems rather difficult, but I did study Latin when I was younger, and I still remember some. Since many of our English words come from Latin roots and are therefore like Italian, it is easy to guess their meaning. The most difficult is conjugating verbs, for there are many different endings. I suppose one gets used to it in time.

Next we concentrated on names of things we could see in the room:

> table *il tavolo*
> friends *gli amici*
> woman *la donna*
> man *l'uomo*
> chair *la sedia*
> clock *l'orologio*
> glass *il bicchiere*
> spoon *il cucchiaio* (this is most difficult to pronounce)
> fork *la forchetta*

Mr. Bartoli said, "Did you know that Italians introduced forks to England?"

"Really?" I asked in surprise, "What did we use before that?"

"Your hands, I think."

I looked at Rev. Houghton, the Pierces, Celia and Dorothea and imagined them using their hands to eat. Since they all think they are proper English ladies and gentlemen, this struck me as quite funny.

"Can you picture them eating with their hands?" I whispered to Mr. Bartoli, mischievously.

Then we both began to laugh. The more we tried not to laugh, the more we were unable to stop. I hid my face with my hand so that the others wouldn't see. I haven't laughed so much for a long time, and it was a good feeling even though my sides did ache from it after.

In spite of trying not to be noticed, Dorothea did notice us laughing. I suppose she always has one eye on me since she is my chaperone.

"What are you finding so funny, Claire?"

"It's my pronunciation; it's quite hopeless," I lied.

We tried to go on, but soon we would start laughing again at some other ridiculous thought.

"Italians also started banks, too. Bank is *banca*," Mr. Bartoli tried to get us back to a serious lesson.

"No, no, please, don't tell me anything else that will start me laughing again," I begged.

"But it's true, and there is nothing funny about it. It was during the Middle Ages. The Medici bank was the largest one," he insisted, ignoring my plea.

"We visited the Uffizi Palace when we were in Florence. That was the Medici's palace wasn't it?" I asked.

"*Si, si,*" he answered.

It was hopeless to be too serious for long. In spite of the laughing, I did learn some Italian today. And even with the rain and not being able to go out, my day was most enjoyable.

Mr. Bartoli was invited to have dinner with us this evening, and he shared the *vino nobile* he had bought at the *cantina* yesterday. Mr. Bartoli sat opposite and a bit down from me, next to Rev. Houghton. When we began dinner, I saw him purposely pick up his fork, pause, and look at me with a mischievous look in his eye, daring me to laugh. I had to look away, or I would be laughing uncontrollably again. Somehow we managed to finish dinner, and the rest of the evening was without further incident.

When Mr. Bartoli was leaving he called to us, "Come quickly! Look! There are visitors in your garden."

Not knowing what to expect, everyone hurried to the door. We looked out and saw a most wonderful sight!

Hundreds of little fairy lights dancing amongst trees and flowers.

"They are *le lucciole* ...fireflies," Mr. Bartoli told us.

"How absolutely beautiful," I said and the others agreed.

Mr. Bartoli has turned out to be different from what I expected. And I wonder, with some misgiving, if I flirted with him today; something I had vowed never to do!

Last night I could not get Mr. Bartoli out of my mind, and it took me some time to fall asleep. I remembered enjoying my Italian class so very much, and he really did look very handsome at dinner.

So, I must admit, I was disappointed to hear that Mr. Bartoli is unable to come today because he has a class at the university. I had been looking forward to seeing him again.

We decided to join Rev. Houghton, who invited us to go with him to the spa at *Chianciano Terme*. The baths there are advertised to be good for one's health, and this is one of the reasons he comes to this area every year. It was interesting, but I think one can do that in England, in Bath, with similar results. The smell of mineral salts is strong and a little unpleasant, although, I did feel relaxed after being there. Once again, I slept very well. Could it be that, as promised by the signs at *Chianciano Terme,* it is because my liver is healthier now?

This morning, Mr. Bartoli came to pick us up at the guest house. This time he was only a few minutes late. It was another beautiful day; the sun was shining, the sky, a clear enamelled blue with a few wispy clouds. We went to see the Church of St. Agnes which is just outside the main city gate, *Porto al Prato*. Again it was a fairly long walk; this time not in the country, but through the town. *Chiesa Santa Agnese* was built in the 16th century and Mr. Bartoli told us that St. Agnes is the Patron Saint of Montepulciano. Above the church's entrance, there is a mosaic of St. Agnes holding a lamb. She is pictured with a lamb because "lamb" in Italian is "*agnello*" which is like "Agnes"; also reminding us that Jesus is the Lamb of God. St. Agnes lived during the reign of Emperor Diocletian in the 4th century, and was tortured and killed because she refused to marry a nonbeliever. Rev. Houghton and the Pierces joined us today, and Rev. Houghton said that St. Agnes is one of the Saints that the Church of England recognizes, too.

While we were walking to the church, I saw a man in a brown habit, a rich chocolate color, on the other side of the road. He seemed to be waiting to meet someone, and I asked Mr. Bartoli about him.

"He is a Franciscan brother. You have heard of St. Francis, yes? He was from Assisi, a town in the province of Umbria. We will go there someday. It is a very interesting town. St. Francis lived in the 11th century, and his father was a wealthy cloth merchant. St. Francis felt that God was calling him to give up his inheritance and live a life of poverty. A few of his friends joined him, and they started a new Order of brothers, called the Order of Friars Minor. Sometimes they are simply called Franciscans."

The Church of St. Agnes is not large, but I liked its arched ceiling and the creamy-coloured marble. At the front is a statue of the Virgin Mary behind the altar. She is wearing a crown of stars with angels at her side, guarding her. Mr. Bartoli said that this statue depicts "The Assumption" or the event in which the Virgin was taken up into heaven.

"Like Elijah and Enoch in the Old Testament she, too, was taken, body and soul, to heaven," he said. I had never heard this before, but Dorothea told us that Protestants do not believe this. That is, we believe it about Elijah and Enoch but not the Virgin Mary. I think it is because the stories of Elijah and Enoch are in the Bible, but the story of Mary being assumed into heaven is not. I asked Mr. Bartoli why Roman Catholics believed this.

"If the Blessed Virgin had died and had been buried, there would be some city or town that would claim to have her relics," Mr. Bartoli explained, "To have the bones of a Saint is a great honor for your city. To have the relics of the Mother of Jesus would be an even greater honor. And yet, no place has ever claimed to have the bones of the Virgin Mary. The early Christians believed that she had been taken into heaven, just as Elijah had. It is part of our Tradition."

Well, this was interesting, indeed, and something I had never heard before.

At the side of the church is a lovely little garden surrounded by an arched gallery. We could only look at it from a side door because it is still a convent, and we were not allowed to go in.

As we walked back through the town, Mr. Bartoli pointed out buildings which have Etruscan burial urns built into the bases of their walls. We could see inscriptions on them; some unusual animals, human figures and flower designs. These urns were found in the countryside, then moved here to be used by the builders. Etruscans lived here many years before the Romans did, so these urns are extremely old, and no one has been able to decipher the inscriptions yet. Some of the buildings are palaces, but other than the Etruscan urns in their foundations, they don't look any different than the other buildings of the town.

Mr. Bartoli explained that Montepulciano means "mountain of *Poliziano*". People who live here are called *Poliziani*. There was a famous Renaissance poet at Lorenzo de Medici's court, Angelo Ambrogini, who was known by the name *Poliziano*.

On our way, we passed some present-day *Poliziani*. A group of older men playing dominoes, laughing at each other's jokes. A young woman hurrying home, her little baby on one hip with a basket of fresh vegetables in her other hand. A group of children returning from school, laughing and chattering as children everywhere do. People smiled at us as if we were old friends because they all knew Mr. Bartoli.

Italian is a musical language; that is the only way to describe its staccato rises and falls. But some of the people speak very loudly, at least when they are outside. People called to each other from their windows above the street. A man unloading a cart of fruit at a stall sang an aria from an opera; I think it was from a Verdi opera. Imagine a fruit vendor who can sing operatic arias! It almost seemed as if we were all part of an opera. I asked Mr. Bartoli why everyone always seems so happy. He said, "We can choose to be cheerful even if life is difficult. Why not laugh and sing when we can?" It sounds like a good philosophy of life. I wish I could make it mine! I think, most of the time, I am too melancholic in nature.

We passed by all kinds of shops: stationery shops with dusty books and beautiful marbled paper; a butcher shop with a smoky smell of cured meat, a wild boar's head above its door; and fish shops with their pungent smells of shrimp, clams and sardines wafting onto the street.

When we turned the next corner we saw *La Pulcinella* (which means "the clown"). He is a little mechanical figure with a funny hat, striking the hours throughout the day on top of a tower. It happened to be noon, and *La Pulcinella* struck twelve loud, clanging chimes, as he has been doing for centuries, I suppose.

Across from *La Pulcinella* is the Church of St. Augustine or *Sant'Agostino*. This church is named after St. Augustine of Hippo, not St. Augustine of Canterbury, the St. Augustine who came to England. I've decided of all the churches we have seen, I like this one best of all. Inside it is so white and smooth, as if it had been carved out of one huge block of the purest marble. Like the Church of St. Agnes, St. Augustine's also has a statue of the Virgin Mary wearing a crown of stars behind the altar, but for some reason, I like this one better.

As we were leaving, a tall man in a long black robe and wide-brimmed hat stopped to speak to Mr. Bartoli. We were introduced to Don Angelo, the parish priest. He is not old, about thirty, and although he speaks only a little English, he seemed genuinely happy to meet us.

We walked back to *Piazza Grande*, and because we were a bit tired, and it was warm, we stopped for *limonate* again. I have wanted to ask why the Virgin Mary seems to be so honored here, sometimes even more than Jesus, but I didn't have to as Dorothea asked instead.

"Mr. Bartoli, why do Italians worship the Virgin Mary more than Jesus?" Dorothea asked rather bluntly, "After all she was just an ordinary person."

"Well I wouldn't say we worship her ... only God should be worshipped. But we do honor and love her. I cannot agree that she was "an ordinary person" either. After all, it is a marvellous thing to have been chosen to be the Mother of our Lord, *sì*? It is true that she is not divine like Jesus, but to say she is an "ordinary person", no, no ... wouldn't God prepare the woman he chose for that great task of being the mother of His Son? We believe that Mary always leads us to her Son. Just as she told the servants at the wedding of Cana, 'Do whatever He asks you to do,' she says the same to us."

"We believe she was a Virgin, but we don't pray to her or have statues of her," Dorothea said and I was glad that she did not pursue that subject any further. I think Mr. Bartoli felt it was wise not to say anymore either. Now I understand why the Virgin is so important in Italy ... surely, it *was* a great honour to have been chosen by God to be the mother of Jesus. But were so many paintings and statues of the Virgin necessary, I wondered, and was Jesus pleased at the attention given to His mother? Perhaps He was, for He must have obeyed the commandment to "honour thy father and thy mother". I always feel pleased when someone tells me what a wonderful person my mother is. Still, I do wonder if some of it is excessive.

After our drink and rest, we ended our day's tour by going into the *Duomo*. As Mr. Bartoli had promised, it *is* much nicer inside than outside but still not as nice as the Church of St. Augustine. The most important art here is the altar piece in rich red, orange and gold by Taddeo di Bartolo. Mr. Bartoli said that, unfortunately, he was not a relative of the artist even though their names are similar. We saw more statues, more paintings; one a beautiful one of the Virgin Mary painted on a gold background, which Mr. Bartoli said is called "The Virgin of the Pillar" as it is on one of the pillars of the Cathedral. I couldn't help thinking about what Mr. Bartoli had said about the Virgin Mary. I also wondered why we Protestants think to have a statue is idolatry, whereas a painting is alright. I have always thought that a statue is considered a "graven" or carved image and that is what is forbidden in the Ten Commandments. But is that what it means? And isn't the end result the same; a representation of someone? We certainly do have statues of our national heroes to honour them. Why, there is one of Lord Nelson in London! We honour him, but we certainly don't worship him. Is it only God, the Father, we are not to portray whereas we can have statues and paintings of Our Lord, who was truly Man, as well as God? I have many questions, but I dare not ask anyone.

By this time, we all felt tired, and the bells of the cathedral were ringing to announce evening Mass. We left, as some women and a few older men hurried up the steps in answer to the heavy chime of the bells.

Lorraine Shelstad

"Why are there mostly women going to Mass? Do Italian men not go to Mass often?" Miss Trent asked. I'm sure she asked more out of interest and not in a critical spirit.

"Most of the men are still at work ... and the younger women, too. Usually they go only on Sundays or early in the morning before they go to work in the fields or the shops," Mr. Bartoli answered.

In any case, I was impressed that this many people were going to Mass when it was a weekday and not Sunday.

∽

By this time, it was late, and James could hardly keep his eyes open. He put down the diary. Soon after his head touched his pillow, he was sleeping soundly. He was beginning to sleep better now than when he first came back home. Still there were some nights when he would wake up suddenly, feeling terror, expecting to see a prison guard standing over him, watching him as he slept. After that, it was difficult to get back to sleep. He wondered how long these after-affects of prison camp would last.

Chapter 6

T he next evening after dinner, James sat in his usual chair, and saw the diary on the table beside it. It was raining out and a bit chilly; a perfect evening to stay in and read. For a moment he wondered why he just didn't look up the page with the bookmark. Did he really care about a young woman's romantic ideas about Italy in the 19th century? Well, it wouldn't take much longer to finish, and some of it was entertaining, he had to admit. He began reading where he had left off the night before.

❧

Friday, March 25, 1898.

Today it rained again. Even though it was only a light refreshing rain, I spent another day in the library *cum* sitting room learning Italian. Mr. Bartoli had me read a passage from Dante's *Il Paradisio* in order to listen to my pronunciation, but after a short while, whatever I was reading, reminded him of something in Italian history. He began to talk, not just about medieval history or the Renaissance, which we are always hearing about, but also the history of more recent times. This was more interesting to me than having to read Italian, even if it was Dante. Mr. Bartoli explained that Italy has only been a unified country since 1870. Why, that is less than thirty years! During medieval times, there were city-states; Florence and Siena, for example. Montepulciano had once been aligned with Siena but since it considered itself to be Siena's equal, it eventually went over to fight with Florence. The Papal States were administered by the Pope. They con-sisted of the area around Rome, and extended across the peninsula, including the province of Umbria, where Assisi is. The southern part had various rulers, including the Holy Roman Emperor, Frederick II.

"For many years, we were under Napoleon's rule; we didn't have a Wellington as you did in England. True, the Bonapartes would have felt more at home in Italy than France ... they were, after all, from Corsica which is nearer Italy, and spoke a dialect closer to Italian than French. When Napoleon had been defeated and exiled, most of Italy was ruled by Austria, except for the Papal States and the two Sicilies. The French Revolution had a great influ-ence on European thinking. The poor, especially, wanted to escape the power of those who took advantage of them. In Italy, there are still farmers who are treated badly by their *padrone*. I'm happy to say my father treats his workers fairly," he paused and then went on, "Now the ideas of Lenin and Marx have became popular. As well, a number of Italian men have joined secret societies; those which have always tried to undermine the Church."

"Secret societies?" I had never heard of these.

"The Carboneri for one. They copied the Freemasons; these you have in England. It seems that even Garibaldi ... you have heard of Garibaldi, yes? ... was a Freemason. The Pope has written about how they threaten religion and undermine morality."

I had heard about Freemasons, but didn't know much about them and had certainly not heard that they threatened religion or morality.

"In 1861, Garibaldi led a group of men who fought to unify the cities of Italy. They started in the south ... in Sicily. Eventually all the territories were united under King Victor Emmanuel II who had been ruling the island nation of Sardegna. This unification is called the *Risorgimento*. Many Italians think that, after all the fighting and sacrifice, it hasn't made much difference. They think we are still not as progressive as other nations."

"But surely you are *more* progressive than anyone else," I teased, "After all Italians introduced forks to the rest of Europe."

"Ah, yes, it is true," he nodded seriously, "But that was during Medieval times. At that time, the city states were progressive; in trade, banking, in political thought and education. Do you know that the first university in Europe was in Bologna? But now people say that we are backward ... in industry, manufacturing and education. In fact, some claim we are a country only good for good wine and Grand Tours."

"But surely you don't think that do you, Mr. Bartoli? Do you believe that unifying the country was a good thing?" I wanted to know what he thought, for politics in Italy seemed to be a subject which interested him a great deal. I was especially pleased that he would discuss history and politics with me, a woman only eighteen years old!

"No, I believe Italy is still a great country, in spite of some problems. I like to look back at the times of the magnificent art, architecture and music. It is true, there are many advantages to being united into one country, but those who fought to unite Italy want the Church ... and the Pope ... to have less power. There are those who even want to do away with the Church! Italy cannot survive without it.

The Church gives us our identity, our art and yes, our soul. Rome is at the center of the Church. But you are English; you cannot understand what I mean."

It seemed that being English, not my youth nor my sex, was my primary fault. Here, I felt I surely had to defend myself and my countrymen. After all, the British Empire is so extant that the sun never sets on it!

"Well, our roots are in the Catholic church, too ... until King Henry VIII declared himself the head of the English Church, we were under the Pope. The Church of England considers itself Catholic but not *Roman* Catholic, and therefore we don't recognize the Pope. Our present Queen, Victoria, who is now the Head of the English Church, believes that religion is important for our country. Surely, if nothing else, being Christian should affect our manners, our laws and how we treat others. I suppose not all English think this way, though. My father says that some people today have rather strange beliefs."

Mr. Bartoli looked at me, smiled and decided we should change the subject to Italian verbs. Maybe he didn't agree with what I had said or he remembered that Dorothea had instructed him not to talk about religion. It is true, of course, that I cannot understand what it is like to be Italian or Roman Catholic.

I learned some more adjectives: *bella (beautiful), brutto (ugly), buono (good)* and how they must agree with the nouns they modify; feminine, masculine, plural or singular. This is more complicated than English, but some words certainly sound like what they mean. *Brutto,* for example, does indeed sound ugly.

Tomorrow we plan to go to Siena. This evening we will retire early in order to get an early start in the morning. Rev. Houghton, the Pierces, Miss Trent, Dorothea and I will be going. Again Mr. Bartoli will be our guide.

This morning was bright and sunny; perfect weather for our trip to Siena. The countryside is so beautiful; after the rain yesterday it looks even greener than before. Plum trees along the roadside are just beginning to flower; they remind me of bridesmaids in pink and white gowns. The green fields beyond the road are already brilliant with blood-red poppies.

We reached Siena by mid-morning. First we stopped at San Domenica, a church where we saw a chapel that had St. Catherine's skull displayed. There is also a portrait of St. Catherine by Andreotti Vanni in the church. I must say the picture looks nicer than her skull, which is almost five hundred years old! I'm not sure why people would want to see someone's skull. I did remember what Mr. Bartoli had said about it being an honor for a town to possess the relics of a saint, so I suppose that is why.

Mr. Bartoli told us about Caterina Benincasa which was St. Catherine's family name. She was the daughter of a wealthy cloth merchant who lived in Siena during the 12th century. Although she did not become a nun, she was a lay Dominican making it possible for her to stay at her home and live with her family. The Dominican Order was started by St. Dominic, a Spaniard, about the same time as the Franciscan Order. Because she was a lay Dominican, she could have married; her family wished her to, but she never did. St. Catherine had visions of Christ and was sought out by many for her goodness and her wisdom. She even wrote to advise Popes and Kings, and surprisingly, they heeded her advice. Imagine, men following the advice of a woman! She convinced Pope Gregory XI that he should leave Avignon in France, where Popes had been for many years, and return to Rome. She believed that it was the rightful place for the Pope who is, after all, the Bishop of Rome.

After seeing *San Domenica* and the *Duomo*, large and dark inside with black and white striped marble, we went to *Il Campo*, Siena's town square. It is not really a square but rather a half-circle, like a huge, pink shell gently sloping into its center. Surrounding *Il Campo* are *The Palazzo Pubblico*, the administrative building of the Sienese republic, and some small shops and restaurants. Next to the *Palazzo Pubblico* is the tower, *Il Torre del Mangia*. Today *Il Campo* was full of sunshine and people.

We entered *Palazzo Pubblico* to see paintings by Ambrogio Lorenzetti on the two walls opposite each other. On one side is the *Effect of Good Government*, which has figures of the Cardinal Virtues: Peace, Prudence, Temperance, Justice, Magnanimity and Fortitude. On the other side of the room, we saw the *Effect of Bad Government* and Tyranny is in charge. This painting has figures representing Avarice, Pride, Vainglory, Cruelty, Treason, Fraud and War. Justice is bound, while robbers roam the city streets. A group of wild-looking men is dragging a woman by her hair. It is a terrible scene, and one I won't soon forget. The message about government is clear: if a country has good government it will have peace in its streets; if a country does not have good government it will have tyranny and crime. Mr. Bartoli said that Italy's government should heed the artist's advice. Rev. Houghton diplomatically added that he thought all governments would benefit from the allegory.

When we went out onto *Il Campo* again, Signore Bartoli told us about something more cheerful, the *Palio*, which began during the Middle Ages and has been held every summer since. Horses and their riders come from all the *contrade* or neighbourhoods to race around Il Campo. Each *contrada*, has a strange name like *Lupo* (wolf), *Aquila* (eagle) and *Drago* (dragon), and has its own colourful flag with its crest on it. Even today, these colorful flags are hanging in the square:

bright greens, reds and yellows. Some have stripes or checks, and all have crests representing their *contrada*. On the day of the race, thousands of people stand around *Il Campo* to watch. Mr. Bartoli says it is very exciting but also dangerous. Everyone cheers for his own neighbourhood to win the prize; a banner with the Virgin Mary embroidered on it. It is claimed that no one has ever died in the race because the Virgin protects them.

"But," Mr. Bartoli admitted, "There are often crimes committed; gambling, cheating, and even bribing, and the Virgin Mary cannot be happy about that."

We stopped and had *gelati*, a frozen dessert made from milk. We were told that it was first made for the Medici family. Others claim that Arabs introduced it to Sicily in southern Italy, and its popularity spread to the north. By this time the sun was blazing hot, so the cool *gelato* was especially good whoever had been the first to make it! Miss Trent mentioned that she had once eaten this in London and Rev. Houghton said that something similar is available in England now. "It is called ice cream," he said, "But it cannot be compared to *gelati* in Italy, which is far more delicious."

Mr. Bartoli pointed out the University buildings where he studies. They are near *Il Campo* and look just like the other buildings on that street. One cannot tell that they are part of a university unless you can read the signs. It is certainly unlike the Colleges of Oxford which have beautiful buildings and spires, green lawns and look like a university is meant to look, in my opinion anyway. The University in Siena began in 1240, and one can study either law or medicine there. Rev. Houghton said that Oxford also began in the 13th century but it is not certain what year, probably a few years later. The University in Bologna is the oldest in the world (I remembered Mr. Bartoli telling me this the other day) probably established in 1048! What is most interesting is that all universities, even Oxford and Cambridge, were established by the Church before the English broke with Rome.

When we had seen almost everything in Siena, Mr. Bartoli said it was time to go back home, and he arranged for a couple of carriages to take us back. But while we were waiting for them, he announced that he had prepared a surprise for us, "We're going to stop for lunch at my home. It's on our way back to Montepulciano."

Shortly after leaving Siena, we turned down a long, narrow road lined with almost-black cypress trees. Mr. Bartoli had the coach stop in front of the two-story house made of ochre-colored stone. It was fairly large with a typical tiled roof, and there were some other buildings nearby, places where animals were kept or where olives were pressed. On either side of the house were groves of silvery-leafed olive trees, hundreds of years old. When we approached, I could see that the main house was u-shaped in the back, and there were several dogs, a goat and some small children playing there. We were led into a shaded garden at the front where a table covered by a cutwork-lace cloth, brilliantly white in the sunshine, was set with blue and yellow dishes of an unusual pattern. A forsythia bush nearby had burst into yellow flowers, and some small, deep-purple irises had just pushed through the damp earth nearby. I could smell lilacs but I couldn't see a lilac bush. The scent reminded me of England in spring and I felt the sudden pain of homesickness.

A slim, elegant-looking lady came out of the house to meet us. Her black hair was pulled back into a neat coil at the nape of her neck, and she was wearing a dove-grey dress with a white lace shawl. Mr. Bartoli greeted her by kissing her on each cheek and introduced us to his mother. He was obviously proud of her, and she looked equally proud of him. I have never thought about this before, but it occurred to me that Jesus may have greeted his mother in a similar way after returning from a journey!

Mrs. Bartoli greeted us in Italian, saying she was happy to meet us, and I was able to answer, "*Molto piacere*" or "I am pleased to meet you." I had just learned this the other day.

I didn't know there were so many different kinds of cheese. Mr. Bartoli told us the *pecarino* is goat cheese and a specialty of this area. We had to try it! I was surprised that I liked it even though it had a strong taste. At least, I ate a little bit. There was some cured boar meat to eat with the cheese and slices of bread so fresh I could still smell the yeast. For our sweet we had a special Siennese cake called *panforte* which Mr. Bartoli had bought earlier that day. It was made of nuts, spices and dried fruit. We were each given a glass of *vin santo,* a sweet, amber-colored dessert wine to sip with our *panforte.* To end our lunch we had coffee but I'm afraid coffee is too bitter for me. It was the first time I had tasted it, and not being accustomed to the taste I couldn't finish mine. I still prefer tea.

Poor Mr. Bartoli, because he was kept busy translating and explaining everything, wasn't able to eat much. Although there was a young maid, who brought things from their kitchen and served, it was Mr. Bartoli who served the coffee to us.

Apart from that coffee, I must say, it was a most enjoyable meal. Sitting in the lovely garden was pleasant and peaceful. The scents of basil and rosemary growing in the garden will always remind me of Tuscany. Everyone, even Dorothea, seemed more relaxed there. As we were leaving I saw the lilac bush, heavy with purple blooms, beside the house. I ran over to breathe in that well-remembered scent. Mr. Bartoli's mother asked the young girl to cut a bouquet for me to take home. They also gave us a huge round of *pecarino* cheese and some of their best olive oil to take back to the guest house.

Mr. Bartoli announced that tomorrow he had arranged for us to go on a *merenda*.

"What is a *merenda?*" We all wanted to know.

"I can't think of the English. It is where you take your food with you and eat outside."

"A picnic!" I cried.

"*Si, si.* A picnic."

I must confess I couldn't eat much at tea that evening. We were still satisfied from our lunch. But I did sleep well after our busy day, and I look forward to the *merenda* tomorrow.

Today (Sunday), after Morning Prayers led by Rev. Houghton, Mr. Bartoli came to the guest house on his way from Mass. He had arranged for a fly to take us and had asked the guesthouse to prepare a picnic lunch. All the guests went on the *merenda*.

Thinking it would be a hot day, I decided to wear my white muslin dress with the lace collar. Nora had done my hair in a different style, and when I passed the mirror in my room, I noticed that my complexion has definitely improved since coming here. I didn't even have to pinch my cheeks to look healthy. I suppose it is all the sunshine and fresh air we are getting.

Mr. Bartoli must have agreed, for when I came out of the guest house, and he took my hand to help me into the carriage, he said, "*Bella, bella,* Miss Ashford. You should always wear white!"

I was pleased by his comment but felt a little embarrassed and Dorothea looked at me strangely.

We had our picnic overlooking *Lago di Chiusi*. Certainly it is a view which rivals anything we have seen thus far. It lay in a hollow; intensely blue and tranquil below us.

Maria Balfour had made a simple but delicious lunch of cheese, preserved meats and bread. She also sent a bottle of Chianti wine and lemonade to drink. The day was perfect in every way.

Later, after we got back, I was writing a letter to Mama and Papa in my room telling them about our trip to Siena and the picnic when Dorothea came to see me.

She asked me how I enjoyed the day, and I said that I'd enjoyed it immensely. She hesitated briefly and asked, "What do you think of Mr. Bartoli?"

"Oh, he's an excellent teacher. You made an excellent choice in securing him. I can speak some Italian already, but my pronunciation is not particularly good."

"Yes, you mentioned that the other day. I mean, what do you think of him ... other than as a teacher?"

"Well, he's been extremely kind and always a gentleman. And he's somewhat handsome, don't you agree?"

What did she expect me to say, I wondered?

"Claire, you must be careful not to like him too much," she said carefully, "And always be on your guard. I suppose I should have warned you before this."

"What do you mean?" I asked with alarm. Was Mr. Bartoli not the person he seemed to be? Had she discovered that my tutor had a secret past? We had been to his house and met his mother, and she seemed to be generous and kind. Mr. Bartoli was always polite, and he was at the university reading law; surely he was someone we could trust.

"Well, I should have told you that you must be wary of Italian men ... well, all Italians, for that matter. They are ... different than we English."

"How do you mean? They certainly seem kind and friendly," I remembered the cheese and flowers we had been given at Mr. Bartoli's home.

"Yes, but their religion ... you know their beliefs about the Pope and Mary ... it makes them behave differently."

"But the art we came here to see ... weren't the artists Roman Catholic? The paintings are often of Mary or Jesus or other stories from the Bible. We believe those stories, too."

"You are still young, Claire, and this is the first time you've been abroad. Not all people are like the English. Here there is a lot superstition mixed in with their religion, for example, the Mass."

"I see."

But I didn't see, for it seemed that these "beliefs" did not affect their behavior or generosity in a negative way. In fact, there was a warmth and joy which I did not always feel even amongst my own countrymen. Sometimes we English have so many unspoken rules on how to act in polite society that we cannot be ourselves; at least until we know someone very well.

"What I mean is that you must not take Mr. Bartoli's compliments too seriously."

"Do you mean when he said I was *bella* this morning? Oh, Dorothea, he only said this to remind me of one of the words I had learned yesterday." Quite frankly, I hoped that this was not his only reason for the compliment and that he had really meant it!

"Well, do remember what I've said, Claire."

"Of course. Thank you, Dorothea," and I kissed her on the cheek. I'm sure she meant well although her ideas seem somewhat old-fashioned at times. She is, after all, responsible for me here.

Chapter 7

I don't know when I got the idea that I wanted to go to Mass. I think it was after I visited St. Augustine's and then especially after Dorothea's warnings. There is something perverse in my nature; I often want to do what I know I'm not supposed to do. I remembered that the *Duomo* has a Mass at 5:00 in the late afternoon and that was the time that everyone at the guesthouse usually rests and prepares for dinner. I have also noticed that young women my age do walk around by themselves on errands, but then I, as a foreigner, would be noticed and people may think it strange to see me on my own. However, I decided to take this chance. I had to know what was so *dangerous* about the Catholic Mass.

It was already past 4:30 and I grabbed my shawl, put on a bonnet and hurried out. I followed the main street, *Il Corso*, and knew all the turns that led to the *piazza*. It had rained earlier. The paving stones were a shiny black, and the air smelled fresh and clean. As I got closer to the *piazza*, the noisy clang of the bells became louder, and my heart beat faster. I hoped that I was not doing something too wrong, although it was rather exciting to be daring for a change. Others were hurrying up the steps beside me; a few smiled but most just ignored me, intent on their own thoughts. To be honest, I was glad to be ignored.

Inside it was cool and dark; the quietness could almost be touched. I felt as if I had stepped into a tomb; not a morbid place, but somewhere completely peaceful. A few people were kneeling and praying, and others were just sitting quietly, waiting. Several people were using the beads they have for prayers; slipping them easily through their fingers, their lips moving silently. No one spoke aloud. Those same people who were often shouting outside had come here to be with God, not to visit. I took a seat near the back but not too far away from others that I would look conspicuous. It was easy to sit in the shadows beside one of the pillars. I could see the altar clearly, for it was brightly lit with candles, and the red and gold painted screen reflected their warm, mysterious glow.

The people sat quietly until the priest came out from the side, and Mass began. Even though I could not understand the readings or the sermon, I did recognize some of the words. As for the rest, I could guess because I remembered some Latin from my schoolroom days. There were parts I did not understand but most of it was similar to what I am used to in the English church. We knelt or stood, and everyone gave their responses at the proper time. At times the people sang ... but there was no organ or other musical instrument ... just the voices of people singing a simple melody. When I heard "*Credo in unem Deum, Patrem omnipotentem* ..." I recognized the Nicene Creed which I had once memorized in Latin. We say the Creed in our church, as well, but in English. So it seems the main things we believe are not so different after all!

Soon it was time to go forward to receive the Host; each person walked up and knelt down and the priest placed the round Host on their tongues. They walked slowly past me, the full range of humanity. A woman with a wrinkled face and the smile of an angel. An old man with a limp making his way slowly to the front. A young woman carrying a plump, happy child followed by a middle-aged woman still wearing her apron. There were a few older men but only two that could be considered *young*; one appeared to be with his mother and the other sat by himself. I remembered Mr. Bartoli explaining that most men were still working in the fields at this time. As the people returned after receiving communion, they seemed to have a look of satisfaction on their faces as if a hunger in their hearts had been satisfied. After a prayer, the priest said "*Ite, missa est*"; the Mass had ended. The people sang another lovely melody; a repeated refrain which included the word, *Signore*. I guessed that *Signore* means "Lord". Everything was simple but beautiful, and again, as I seem to feel so often here, I felt at home. After the candles were extinguished, clouds of smoke lingered in the darkness, and the heavy scent of incense caught in the back of my throat. I left as inconspicuously as I had come.

Outside in the *piazza* the late afternoon sunshine washed everything with a pale gold light. Walking home more slowly than when I had come, I noticed some little boys with dirty faces, barefoot and dressed in ragged clothes. They were bouncing a ball off the ancient wall of an equally ancient building. They seemed so happy even though they were obviously poor. A group of young men outside a café saw me, called out something and then laughed at their own joke. I recognized the word *Inglese*; obviously they were talking about me. They were possibly being impolite. In any case, I walked more quickly, thinking it was better not to acknowledge their remarks or even look at them. I remember thinking that it seemed not all the young men were working in the fields at this time. I was also a bit worried that someone at the guest-house had discovered my absence. What would I say?

I came to the street where I could look down over the wall onto the same view I have from my window. I saw those familiar fields, this time the mist of dusk was a golden light diffusing the very air around me. In the distance were the hills; different shades of purple and mauve and soft violet, folded layer upon layer. How beautiful it was. And how beautiful the Mass had been. Certainly as beautiful as any service I have been to in my own parish church in England, even though I hadn't understood it all.

As I turned the last corner, I saw a couple walking ahead of me. I was surprised when I realized that it was Mr. Bartoli, walking with a young woman. Her dark hair fell in soft curls and was worn loose to her shoulders. She wore a white blouse with long, full sleeves and a plain, long dark skirt. I could see the side of her face as she turned to talk and she was very pretty. They were talking and laughing together with the ease of those who knew each other well. As they were walking in the same direction as I was, they didn't notice me. I had not seen them at the *Duomo*. Were they returning from Mass at *Sant'Agostino*, which was nearby? I slowed my pace slightly to make sure I would not be seen, and soon I turned into the narrow street which led to the guesthouse.

Dorothea was right; I should not like Mr. Bartoli too much. I had no reason to think he liked me in any particular way, and now it seemed probable that he had an attachment already. I felt a sad, hollow feeling inside of me. At the same time, the peace I had experienced during Mass did not leave me.

Dorothea saw me come in as she was coming down the stairs.

"Wherever have you been, Claire? I was just at your room."

"My room was too warm. I couldn't bear it, so I went out for a walk," I lied, adding to my guilt.

"You walked in the streets alone?" she asked incredulously.

"Yes." That at least was true.

I ran up the stairs before she could ask any more questions and I would have to tell more lies. The sweet smell of incense clung to my dress, and I hoped Dorothea hadn't noticed it. I just had time to change and freshen for dinner. I wasn't hungry and was sure I wouldn't be able to eat much.

"Actually, we are missing out on the best part of Italian life," Rev. Houghton was saying as I entered the sitting room, "Tonight I suggest we go out for a walk after dinner. It is what the Italians do."

"Isn't that what they call *passeggiata*?" asked Mr. Pierce, who does not often contribute much to the conversation but, occasionally, likes to show off his knowledge. Mrs. Pierce smiled proudly at her husband.

So, it was decided that we would all go out for a walk after dinner and for the second time that day I walked to *Piazza Grande*. I would have rather stayed at home. What if I saw Mr. Bartoli and the young woman again?

There was certainly a liveliness in Montepulciano's streets that is not there in daytime. Families walked together; couples strolled, glancing shyly at each other and groups of young people joked and laughed, noisily enjoying themselves. I was afraid to look at those couples walking in the half-darkened *Via Corso* in case they turned out to be Mr.Bartoli and the pretty woman. When we got to the *piazza* we decided to have *gelati*, even though the evening air was cool.

At one corner, a small, dark-skinned man was playing a cheerful tune on a concertina. Was he from some part of Italy or was he from a neighboring country? Was he one of the gypsies that we had heard about? I liked his happy music and, if I had been in better spirits, I would have felt like dancing.

Parents were showing off their babies: all the little girls were *bella* and all the little boys were *bravo*. How proud they were of their children! How lovely it was to see families strolling together in the *piazza*!

I did not see Mr. Bartoli and the young woman again, but I still could not help wondering who she was.

I didn't sleep well last night. It was too warm in my room and I had much to think about: the Mass and Mr. Bartoli and what Dorothea had said about not trusting Italians. When Dorothea spoke to me, I didn't think I felt anything special for my tutor. But when I saw him with the beautiful girl, I realized that I *did* like him more than I had been willing to admit, even to myself. I did enjoy talking to him and laughing together, but was that love? I think women are often attracted to men who are kind to them ... and Mr. Bartoli had been kind. Yes, that was all it was; just kindness.

This morning, Mr. Bartoli sent word that he won't be able come for a few days, as he has special lectures at the university. I must admit this time I will be glad not to see him for a while. I can't really ask him about the woman he was with, and I'm not sure if I can act the same when I am with him as I did before. I wonder if he will mention her to me. He probably won't feel obligated to do so. Why would he when he doesn't even know that I saw them?

We heard that tomorrow other guests are arriving at *Albergo Vittoria*. It will be good to have more people here, and I still hope that someone my own age will come.

Everyone seemed to be doing something on their own today. I refused to give in to melancholy this time and decided to get out my water colors to paint my favorite view from the garden wall. I wasn't sure if I could mix enough different greens and browns to match those in the fields and vineyards below but, in any case, I managed to amuse myself most of the day. I worked feverishly, as if working would help me forget everything else. I stopped only for our meal at noon, then afternoon English-style tea which we always have if we are not out touring somewhere. For some reason, I felt I had to keep my mind occupied and not think of Mr. Bartoli. Rev. Houghton came to look at my painting and sat down to chat. He gave me some expert advice about the colors I was using, but he thought I had captured the mood of Tuscany very well. He especially liked the way I had used light and shadows. He said although this use of *chiaroscuro* was good, it was not quite as good as that of the Italian masters of the Renaissance! Of course, he was teasing me. He is most amiable and knows a lot about Italy. He comes to Tuscany to enjoy the peaceful countryside, healthy air and the nearby spa. Although he doesn't know many Italians personally, he seems to genuinely like them and has no criticisms of anyone, at least not to me. I decided to ask him the question that was bothering me.

"Rev. Houghton," I began, "Do you think that Italians are very different from the English?"

"Well, I've travelled in several countries, and although people speak different languages and have different customs and religions, they are all alike in the basic ways. They all love, and hate and feel joy and sadness. There are few people in the world who do not love their children and their parents. Everyone has problems and questions about life. To answer your question, no, Italians are not that different than the English. There are good people and bad people here – as there are in England. We like to think that we English are more polite, more honest and more trustworthy than others, but I suspect that the Italians think that about themselves, too."

"Yes, I think you are right."

"You know, Claire, some people get their ideas of Italians from novels they've read ... like Mrs. Radcliffe's books. In her books, the Italians are always villains."

"I've never read any of her books," I admitted.

"It's just as well. I would say travel is a better teacher than a novel. Are you enjoying your study of the Italian language?"

"Oh, yes, much better than I expected I would." Rev. Houghton smiled at this.

Just then Mr. Pierce joined us, and the topic changed to the fine weather we are enjoying today.

Today a letter arrived from home. I was happy to hear news of everyone. George is busy with his studies and has not been home for some time. The girls are enjoying dancing parties with their friends but are not concentrating on their studies. Mother is hoping the weather will change for the better before I return to England, and Father is busy at his work, as usual. They wonder how I am and hope that I am enjoying Italy and learning about Italian art and music. They look forward to my return.

And the new guests have arrived. They are Mrs. Fillmore, a widow, who is travelling with her son, Mr. Richard Fillmore. Or it would be more correct to say Mr. Fillmore is travelling with his mother. When I saw Mrs. Fillmore, I was immediately reminded of Charlotte Bronte's description of the typical English country lady: "...they all have a certain expression stamped on their features, "I know that I am the standard of what is proper." Mrs. Fillmore is a tall woman with a commanding appearance and a fine figure. For dinner tonight she wore a lovely, lilac, silk gown which suited her white hair and clear, blue eyes. She is definitely someone who is not to be trifled with, and when I'm near her I will try to be most agreeable. Her son appears to be about twenty-five, of medium height with sandy-colored, thinning hair and a rather beak-like nose. He is not unpleasant looking, but certainly not what one would call handsome. They live near London, and Mr. Fillmore is preparing for some ministry, I'm not sure what, it could be a career in the church. This is their first trip to Italy, but they have already been to Venice, Florence and Rome. It is a shame, though, that they have missed many of our outings here.

They will, however, be joining us on our trip to Assisi tomorrow which is to be an overnight trip. Because Mr. Bartoli won't be with us, Rev. Houghton has offered to be our guide and has arranged everything.

Chapter 8

J ames had made arrangements to meet with some of his men; those who had been in the prison camp with him. They had gone through the same nightmares, had seen their comrades die and had felt the same anxieties coming back to England. But when they got together, they didn't moan or talk about their troubles. These things were barely mentioned. Instead, they joked and laughed about the things and people they remembered. The funny guards who shouted "Speedo! Speedo!" to make them work faster. The rude nicknames that they had given some of Japanese officers. The one officer who seemed kinder than the others and showed everyone pictures of his children. The terrible food they were expected to eat. Sometimes what they talked about wasn't even funny, but they laughed anyway. They didn't want to remember the bad things, so they didn't talk about them.

When he returned home after and sat down in his library, he felt better about life and was ready to continue reading the journal of Claire Ashford.

෴

Rev. Houghton knows a lot about Italian history, especially that of Tuscany and Umbria. Of course, he does not know as much as Mr. Bartoli, but we are fortunate to have him as our guide today.

Just outside of Assisi we stopped for the noon meal at a *trattoria* with a lovely dining room that reminded me of a cozy English inn. We feasted on roast lamb, an assortment of vegetables and for dessert, cheese and fruit. This was a nice change from the roast chicken we usually get at the guesthouse. During our meal Rev. Houghton told us of St. Francis, as he thought we needed to know the story in order to appreciate our visit to Assisi.

Francis Bernadone was the son of a wealthy cloth merchant in Assisi. (It seems that a lot of saints are children of cloth merchants. I wonder why.) He was born in the 12th century and typically, Francis had a group of rowdy friends, somewhat like Shakespeare's Romeo, I imagine. After a short time as a knight fighting in the wars between the nearby cities, he became very ill and almost died. During this illness, Francis had a spiritual experience and decided that in order to truly live the gospel as Jesus intended one must live in poverty. He stripped off his expensive clothes and stood stark-naked in Assisi's streets as he renounced his father's fortune. This made his father so angry with Francis that he disowned him. But Francis was not discouraged and from then on went about the town in simple beggar's clothing.

Once, while praying, Francis heard God speak to him. "Rebuild My Church," he heard someone say clearly. He understood this to mean that God wanted him to repair the broken-down church, *San Damiano*, where he was praying, and he started to do just that; rebuild its walls, stone by stone. A few of his friends joined him and they lived by begging their daily food from the townspeople. Dressed in their simple robes, they prayed and preached the gospel in the area around Assisi. Eventually they went to Rome for an audience with Pope Innocent III to ask him for recognition of their new Order. When he heard Francis' story, Pope Innocent realized that Francis had been chosen by God to "rebuild the Church" in a metaphorical or spiritual way rather than a physical way, and approved their Order. The Pope agreed that the Church needed some changes, especially the present view of riches and poverty. Francis called this new order the Order of Friars Minor because he wanted to emphasize that they were the "least important" in God's kingdom. The young daughter of another of Assisi's noble families, Clare, and at this point of his story Rev. Houghton smiled at me, heard Francis preach about Jesus. She, too, left her wealthy family to become a disciple of Francis. Later, her sister also followed her. Since Clare could not join the same Order as the men, she began an Order of women known as the Poor Clares. Members of both Orders take vows of poverty, chastity and obedience, and they still exist today, like the monk we had seen in Montepulciano.

There are many stories of St. Francis making friends of animals, and in one story he even preaches to a flock of birds. Dorothea relegated this to "the usual superstition of the Italians", and I must admit I find some of these stories difficult to believe. Rev. Houghton said they may be legends that were told about St. Francis after he died but, he reminded us, God can still perform miracles, and we should not dismiss them too easily. Shortly after Francis' death in 1226, the Church declared him a Saint.

After our meal, we went to the Basilica of St. Francis which sits on a piece of high ground overlooking a valley. The basilica is large, and inside the walls are covered with murals painted by the artist, Giotto, which tell the story of St. Francis' life. The scene of St. Francis preaching to the birds was included and was so lovely I could almost believe the story. Someone wondered if St. Francis, who had so enthusiastically espoused poverty, would be unhappy with such a grand basilica. I disagree. Since it is for the glory of God and not his own, somehow I don't think he would mind.

Outside we saw many Franciscan monks walking in pairs, hurrying down the streets; their brown robes flapping and the white ropes around their waists swinging. Were they late for Mass or did they always walk that way, I wondered?

Next we visited St. Clare's church; she also was declared a saint and merited her own church. It was also beautiful. In fact, I think I prefer it to the Basilica of St. Francis. I shall never forget the many-arched ceiling; rich sapphire blue sprinkled with gold stars.

Our last stop was the *Church of San Damiano;* the church where St. Francis was praying when Jesus spoke to him from the cross. The cross of *San Damiano* is a rather unusual shape, wider at the ends, and decorated with brightly-colored paintings of Jesus and his disciples. Crosses similar to this can be bought in shops in the town, and although I wanted to buy one I did not. I knew that Dorothea would not be pleased.

We stayed overnight at a guesthouse run by Sisters. Dorothea seemed uncomfortable being there and was somewhat annoyed with Rev. Houghton for arranging to stay at a "papist" place. It was clean, though plain in decor, and our dinner was extremely tasty. In any case, I don't think there were many choices of places to stay. The city is crowded with pilgrims, and although there are many hotels and guest houses, I doubt if there are any that are not "papist". It didn't interfere with my rest; I slept well, possibly because I was exhausted from walking in the fresh air.

We left to return to Montepulciano this morning after a light breakfast. As we didn't have to rush, the trip was pleasant, and I enjoyed looking at the rolling hills and brilliant green fields that we passed. In some fields, groups of men and women were cutting the first hay of the season and tossing it into wagons. By late morning, the sun above was hot, and the workers we saw looked tired and thirsty.

We had to hire two carriages as we are now a group of eight! Dorothea and I travelled with Mrs. Fillmore and her son. Mr. Fillmore attends a Methodist chapel and even though they are from different denominations, he and Dorothea seemed to be in agreement on many issues. In fact, they enjoyed discussing various doctrines of Christianity the entire trip! Mrs. Fillmore seemed interested at first but eventually dozed off, and I entertained myself by looking out at the magnificent scenery. I didn't listen to the conversation as it didn't interest me. I also wanted to think about what I had seen yesterday and the lives of St. Francis and St. Clare. Once I caught Mr. Fillmore staring at me. I suppose he thought me quite rude not to take part in the conversation.

We arrived at the guesthouse just in time for a light supper, and then we retired.

Mr. Bartoli came today. He seemed rather distracted and gave me a test. I had to write for almost an hour. I did not do well at all because I hadn't had a chance to revise beforehand. After discussing my errors on the test, Mr. Bartoli surprised me by saying,

"Someone told me that you were at Mass at the *Duomo* a few days ago."

I think I blushed a little at being found out.

"I suppose I should have guessed someone would mention it to you. But please don't tell Dorothea. She doesn't know."

Mr. Bartoli opened his palms with a kind of shrug and looked up as if to say "What were you thinking of?" but instead he simply asked, "Why did you go?"

"After some remarks of Dorothea's I wanted to go and see for myself what it was like."

"Her remarks were negative?"

"Well ...perhaps a little," I admitted.

"Yes, many English are critical of the Church."

"And what do Italians think of the English?" I asked. He thought for a while and then answered, rather too honestly, I thought.

"We feel sorry for them because they are separated from the true faith."

"Oh." I didn't know what else to say and was surprised that anyone would pity the English at all. I was also astonished that anyone would feel so certain that their faith was the only true one. Do we do the same, I wonder?

"And did you like the Mass?"

"It didn't seem much different than what I'm used to in my parish church at home. But as it was in Latin, I didn't understand all that was said."

"And the Italian? It is evident from your test you didn't understand much of that either!" Mr. Bartoli took the opportunity to remind me of my deficiency in his language, too. He did not seem to be in his usual good humor. Was he angry that I had gone to Mass or was it something else?

"I would have done better had you warned me that I was to have a test," I answered a little defiantly, and then I switched back to the previous subject, "Was it wrong of me to go to Mass?"

"Wrong to go to Mass? No, no, of course not. Maybe it is wrong to deceive Miss Weston though."

I suppose I blushed again a little at this and nodded, but I think he understood it would not help matters to tell her.

"I have not seen you since your trip to Assisi either. What did you think of Assisi?"

"I liked it very much. Rev. Houghton told us more of the story of St. Francis on our way there. He also told us about St. Clare. You didn't mention her to me the other day."

"No, I didn't tell you about her. In Italian, her name is *Santa Chiara*. Should I call you that, *mia bella Chiara?*"

"It's a lovely name in Italian, but perhaps it would be best to call me Claire when others are present."

"Ah yes .... especially Miss Weston."

"Well everyone, but yes, especially Miss Weston," I suppose my expression was rather comical as he laughed, the dark cloud disappeared from his face. His mood had suddenly changed.

I knew it was highly improper to mention seeing him with a young woman, but I wanted so badly to know who she was. The fact that he was in a better mood encouraged me.

"When I was returning from Mass, I saw you walking with a young woman," I tried to sound nonchalant about it, "She was very pretty."

"It must have been someone else you saw," he answered, "I wasn't walking with any woman."

I could not believe my ears! Was he lying to me? I hadn't been mistaken; it was most definitely him I had seen.

"Alright, *Chiara*, let's review some verbs that you have not remembered." The subject had been changed.

Why did he call me *mia bella Chiara* if he does not mean it? Why does he feel he has to lie to me? I am wondering if Dorothea is right, after all, about not trusting Italian men.

It seems that after rushing around to see many places in the past weeks, we are now just resting. Strange that, although I felt tired when I was home in England, here we have been so busy, and I have not felt the least bit tired. When I mentioned this to Celia Trent, she suggested it may have been boredom, and not tiredness, I had felt at home. She said that this had been the case with her once, and that is why she had thought of it. I think that she may be right.

After Morning Prayers (as it is Sunday again); Dorothea, Miss Trent and I walked to a small garden at the end of the street. The scent of early roses and lilies was almost overwhelming and caused me to feel a strange melancholy. We found two old wooden benches at the far end where we could sit and chat about our families, what we liked about Italy, and what we missed of home and England in general. It was all very pleasant. The more I know of Celia Trent the better I like her. She acts in a natural way and does not put on airs at all, although I suppose she could, as her family is fairly prominent in English society. This is the Pierces' first visit to Italy and is also *her* first trip abroad, so she is not at all jaded in her outlook.

We were chatting about Lord Byron (I find his poetry most romantic), and Miss Trent confided, "I heard that Byron had many mistresses while he was here in Italy!"

"But surely his wife was with him at the time, wasn't she?" I asked incredulously.

"I don't know. Apparently he led a completely dissolute life. He could get away with it here in Italy, I suppose; his family in England was none the wiser."

"And his friends were just as bad, so they didn't care," Dorothea added. I was surprised that Dorothea knew anything about Lord Byron's sinful life.

Our conversation about Lord Byron and his mistresses was brought to an abrupt end as we saw Mr. Fillmore coming to join us. I suppose it was not a suitable subject for the Lord's Day anyway! We invited him to join us, which he seemed bent on doing, invited or not. He told us that after he finishes his studies, he plans to go to China as a missionary with a Missionary Society. This was, indeed, news to us all.

"You may find it extravagant that someone who plans to be a missionary would come to Italy on "a Grand Tour" first, but my mother insisted I should see something of the Continent before going to the Orient. She doesn't share my Methodist faith, so she doesn't think I should go to "the ends of the earth" to preach the Gospel. I suspect she is hoping that this trip will cause me to change my mind. However, I am determined to do what I think is God's will for me."

We had a lot of questions to ask him about the Far East, especially the hardships and dangers he will no doubt face. He is willing to do so in order to bring the Gospel to the Chinese people.

"I have read something about the Chinese people," Celia began, "They have beautiful art, pottery, silk, and tea, all of which we benefit from in England. It seems that they are already quite civilized and moral. Do you hope to transform the Chinese people into Englishmen, Mr. Fillmore?"

"Of course not. We have been commanded by our Lord to "go into all the world and preach the gospel". That is what I propose to do. I will teach them about God, even peoples who are civilized need to know Him. Although, I suppose the gospel will change some of their culture; it is inevitable."

Of the three of us, Dorothea was the most interested, as she often helps to raise funds for Missionary Societies and already knows a great deal about them. I tried to be pleasant and take part in the conversation this time, remembering that I had not done so on our return from Assisi.

Soon it was time for us to go back to the guesthouse for our dinner. I didn't really feel all that hungry. I am still upset at Mr. Bartoli's attitude towards me; mostly that he felt it necessary to lie to me. He surely has no reason to be dishonest, for he doesn't know how I feel about him. Why can he not just tell me that he is engaged, if that is the case?

Today (Monday), Mr. Bartoli took us to see the house where Saint Roberto Bellarmine had lived. Bellarmine was a Jesuit priest who was born in Montepulciano in 1542 and was eventually appointed a Cardinal by the Pope. The Jesuits are another Religious Order started by St. Ignatius, a Spaniard, in the 16th century. Cardinal Bellarmine was a friend of Galileo and was also interested in astronomy. Although eventually, Galileo was put under house arrest and excommunicated, it apparently was not because of his discoveries about the earth revolving around the sun, but for his disobedience in writing a book about these discoveries. The Pope wanted him to wait until he had more proof that his theories were correct. Galileo remained a Catholic even after his arrest, however, and his daughter was a nun. Excommunication sounds so dreadful, but it really means that he was not able to take part in the sacraments, which I suppose to a Romanist, is rather serious.

"The real purpose of excommunication is to bring people to repentance," Mr. Bartoli explained.

Roberto Bellarmine was declared a saint after his death, for it seems one has to die before becoming a saint, which is a great pity! We couldn't go inside the house for people still live there, but we were able to see the outside and peek into the courtyard through the open door.

We went to another church nearby; the *Church of Gésu*. I don't like it nearly as well as the others we have seen. The interior is more ornate (baroque, I think is the term used) than the others and yet outside, except for a cross on top, it looks just like the houses crowded on both sides of it.

In the mornings, at street corners, there are tables piled with produce from the surrounding farms; stacks of brown eggs, leafy wild greens tied together in bunches, green and white spring onions in neat rows, and herbs that, when touched, give off lemony scents. Most vendors are women, wearing white cotton blouses and full, long, dark skirts with aprons. A few are men, their faces lined and darkened from working outside. They seem to always be cheerfully joking with those who come to buy their produce.

Every time we walk down the streets of Montepulciano, people greet Mr. Bartoli. He seems to be known and liked by all, young and old. They smile and chat with him, but I understand only a little of what is said, and I don't think that anyone in our group understands very much, with the exception of Rev. Houghton.

Today, I tried to avoid looking at Mr. Bartoli directly and stayed near Miss Trent. She and I walked and laughed together, and I'm trying to act as if nothing has changed.

We came to one small square where we saw many notices edged in black attached to the stone walls. Mr. Bartoli explained that these are notices of people who have died recently. This way everyone in town will know and will be able to go the funeral Mass.

A few days ago we saw a procession of people dressed in black following a coffin and led by a small boy in a white, lacy gown carrying a crucifix. Behind him came the priest in his long, black cassock. A large group of family and friends followed. At the very end of the procession, was a small band of men playing musical instruments. They played a slow march that sounded terribly sad and mournful and, frankly, a bit off-key.

Later in the day, Dorothea and I went to buy more gifts for our friends and families. Miss Trent accompanied us as she also needs to buy gifts for her family before she returns. We had bought a few things already; a lovely little painting of the Italian countryside for my mother and father, the pair of soft chamois leather gloves for my mother, the gold watch chain for my father and gold chains for each of my sisters, all of which I bought in Florence. I also have the water color that I did of the Chianti Valley. I may give that to George. Today I found some marbled paper for my sisters, and I bought some for myself, too. I wanted to find something else for George, but he is difficult to buy for. I looked for a wedding gift for Elsa and Andrew and finally found a mosaic of the *Basilica of the Madonna di San Biagio* at a small studio near the *Piazza Grande.* The tiny pieces of stone are set so well it looks almost like a painting. All in all, I am pleased with what I bought.

This evening after dinner, we were gathered in the sitting room as usual, but tonight the conversation turned to a more interesting topic. Although I hadn't listened to Dorothea and Mr. Fillmore's conversation about religion on our journey back from Assisi, I was interested in tonight's conversation. I think this was mostly because Rev. Houghton was present and he is more of an authority.

It is indeed unusual to have discussions on such "sensitive" topics as religion and politics, especially when ladies are present. Men may have discussions of controversial subjects when they retire to their smoky rooms and drink brandy, but we ladies don't often get to hear them.

"You must admit, Rev. Houghton, that the Roman Church is a complete picture of the apostate church we read about in Revelation and that it is the whore of Babylon," Mr. Fillmore was saying as we ladies entered.

"I can't agree with you, Mr. Fillmore. Cardinal Newman once thought as you do when he was an Evangelical in the English Church. Later he met some Romanist priests that he thought were perfect models of Christianity, and he changed his mind."

"No doubt. He left the Church of England of his youth and joined the Roman Church. Many have called him a heretic, and so I believe, he is."

"I think as he read what the Church actually believed, he was surprised at the perfect sense it all made. Actually, I read that it was the writings of the Church Fathers that changed his mind. I saw him once, at Oxford, shortly before he was made a Cardinal," Rev. Houghton added as an afterthought, "Did you ever see him in Birmingham, Mr. Pierce? He was at the Oratory there, you know."

"I know where the Oratory is, but I've never been there and I didn't ever see Cardinal Newman. I suppose our paths just didn't cross," Mr. Pierce answered.

"What did Cardinal Newman say regarding the Romanist teaching that the bread and wine actually become the body and blood of Jesus?" Dorothea rashly plunged into the men's conversation.

"Well, he was surprised to find that many of the Church Fathers took that for granted. Do you find that doctrine difficult to believe, Miss Weston?" Rev. Houghton turned to her.

"Yes, I do. It's impossible and quite superstitious ... a lot of mummery," answered Dorothea firmly.

"Isn't the belief in the resurrection of Jesus also difficult to believe? That we share with the Romanists," Rev. Houghton pointed out.

"Well, *that* is a miracle central to our faith and is clearly in the Bible," interjected Mr. Fillmore.

"And that is precisely why the Romanists also believe in the miracle of bread and wine becoming the Body and Blood of Christ. This is also in the Bible. Jesus said several times 'This is my Body'," Rev. Houghton added.

"Yes, but surely he meant it in a metaphorical way."

"Who can tell? Some disciples left him because they found it as shocking as you do. Yet Jesus did not try to talk them into returning by saying that he meant "body and blood" metaphorically," Rev. Houghton continued.

Dorothea tried to add something, but the men had taken over the discussion again. From then on she only nodded enthusiastically when Mr. Fillmore made a comment.

"Are you thinking of following Newman then, Rev. Houghton? Perhaps you, too, will be a Cardinal someday,"

Mr. Fillmore said. It seemed he had nothing more convincing to say on the topic of transubstantiation and reverted to sarcasm.

"Well, I've thought of it; becoming a Romanist, not a Cardinal, that is. But I find I'm too English to move completely away from Canterbury just yet," Rev. Houghton laughed to ease the tension in the room, "I think the most difficult hurdle for the English is the Pope ... especially an Italian one! After all, we even had one of our Kings sign the Magna Carta so he wouldn't have too much power. We like to have a say in how we are governed. The Americans are like us."

"Well, I think all creeds are the same. All religions may be true, even those who do not believe in any god at all." This was Mr. Pierce's first contribution and put him in the party of the modernists which is becoming a popular view nowadays.

"Now that I can't agree with. Either there is a God or there isn't. We may not be able to prove either, but ultimately they cannot both be true," Rev. Houghton argued.

"And there, *I* can agree with you, Rev. Houghton," Mr. Fillmore nodded.

Mr. Pierce looked slightly embarrassed for he seemed to be out-numbered. But since his relativist view was gaining popularity in England and he was generally good-natured, he took it in his stride and held no hard feelings. I think, in any case, religion is not one of his pet topics, and he isn't at heart an argumentative person. At that, the discussion came to an abrupt end.

Rev. Houghton's statements were most interesting, and his calm manner and his logic impressed me. I thought of my own parents, my mother in particular. She was certainly faithful to the Church of England, and we never missed a Sunday at church, unless we were ill. But her religion was translated into doing works of charity rather than theological discussions. In fact, religion for her seemed to be summed up in being an obedient wife, a good mother and a faithful citizen. Is this then the essence of Christianity to the majority of English people? Would we ever have had a St. Francis who gave up everything, his inheritance and even marriage, to live as Jesus had taught? What about Mr. Fillmore? Is he an English St. Francis, giving up everything to go to China?

Today, (Tuesday) we travelled to the nearby town of Pienza. Mr. and Mrs. Pierce did not go because they felt too tired, but the others did.

Again our trip was pleasant, and we passed several wagons filled with peasants going to their work in vineyards and hayfields. They waved happily and were laughing and joking with each other. Some were singing. If it hadn't been for thinking of my falling out with Mr. Bartoli, I could have been completely happy.

We reached Pienza early in the day and found it most interesting. Much of Pienza was designed for and built by Pope Pius II, a pope during the 15th century. His family, the Piccolomini family, exiled itself to a nearby village after a military defeat of Siena. When he became Pope he designed and re-built the entire town, naming it Pienza. I thought the cathedral itself was not that memorable, but we peeked into a small, dark Franciscan Church nearby, which is even older than the city. To the side, there was a stand with many candles that people had lit for prayer. The warm glow of the candles weeping tears of wax for sick grandparents, or wayward sons is a sight I won't soon forget. It made me want to light a candle, too, but I dared not.

Like Montepulciano, the streets of Pienza are steep, but here the houses are more charming, smaller cottages of creamy-colored stone. Brilliant red flowers grow beside the steps or pink roses climb haphazardly outside the walls. How I would love to live in a town like this! However, I think it might get tiring climbing the streets. I did notice, though, that even the older people who live here, walk those same cobblestone roads without any problem. Does one get accustomed to it?

It seems we always found Mr. Fillmore walking beside us; Miss Trent and myself. I am wondering if he is interested in getting to know her better. I wouldn't be surprised; she is so charming.

We stopped for some refreshment in the *piazza*, and then we started back to Montepulciano early in the afternoon.

When we arrived back at the guesthouse, I went out to the garden to write about our day in Pienza. It was cool there, and the garden is lovely with pale yellow and white flowers blooming. Mr. and Mrs. Pierce were talking to Miss Trent, asking her about the trip to Pienza. Shortly after, Mr. Fillmore came over to where I was sitting.

"This garden has many lovely flowers, but you, Miss Ashford are indeed the loveliest," he exclaimed. It seemed like a silly thing to say, I thought. He asked if he could join me, and I had no choice but to say, "Yes" although I would have preferred to be alone. After a few comments about our trip to Pienza he surprised me by asking, "Have you ever thought about going to the Mission field, Miss Ashford?"

"No, I never have," I answered honestly.

"Well, I think you have the character and gifts to be a missionary."

I don't know how he would know of my gifts and I've said very little about my beliefs. In fact, I've said very little to him at all. As for my character, I would have thought he would have been rather disappointed in it.

"I wonder if you would be interested in this book? I'd be pleased if you would read it." And he handed me a small, brown book. "*On the Heathen*" was written in gold letters on its spine.

"Thank you," I said out of politeness but frankly the book did not look particularly interesting to me. I admit I would rather read romantic novels or poetry than books of a devotional nature.

"I know that you haven't known me long, but I would like to remain friends and hope that I might call on you once we are back in England."

"But you will be preparing to go to China soon, won't you? Surely you shall be too busy."

"Not at all. One should never be too busy to call on old friends. And it will be some time before I leave for the Far East," he assured me with a confident smile which left me rather disturbed. I have an ominous feeling that Mr. Fillmore's interest is in me and not Celia Trent as I first thought.

We do not have very many days left here in Montepulciano. In some ways, I would be glad to be leaving sooner and not have to give any excuses to Mr. Fillmore or try to avoid him. I will be happy to see my own family again, too. But I will be sad to leave the others; Miss Trent, Rev. Houghton and yes, even Mr. Bartoli. Although it is better to be leaving him, since I am not certain he can be trusted.

Today turned out to be a most remarkable day with more surprises than yesterday, if that is possible.

It was a cloudy day and looked as if it would rain, so it was decided we would stay inside, at least for the morning. We thought that if the sun came out later, we could go for a short excursion.

Mr. Bartoli had me read some Italian poems in order to correct my pronunciation. He said that my pronunciation has greatly improved! I was being fairly cold in my manner towards him, but he seemed neither to notice nor care.

Later, Mr. Bartoli announced to us that he has to go away to Milan and will leave early Friday morning. It seems he will be doing some of his studies at the University of Milan now and will be there for several months. The others then began to discuss Milan and what they knew of it. Mr. Bartoli told me, when the others were talking amongst themselves, that he is a member of the *Società della Gioventù Cattolica Italiana* or Italian Catholic Youth Society. Being in Milan will give him the opportunity to meet with other members there. The Society is a group which supports the Pope and, since Catholics are not to take a direct part in the present government, this group protests any anti-Church activities that the government undertakes. Their protests are made by writing pamphlets or protesting in marches. They are not much different than Newman and the Oxford Group. They also wrote pamphlets to publicize their thoughts about the Church of England and its role in the country. I asked him if there would be any danger.

"If I am doing what God wants me to, the danger is of no consequence," he answered simply, "We must do what we can."

Later the sun did come out, and Mr. Fillmore, Mr. Bartoli, Dorothea, Miss Trent and I went out for a short walk to the square near the Church of St. Augustine and *La Pulcinella*. I heard it chime for the last time before we leave, and that did make me feel sad.

As we were standing in *Piazza Michelozzo*, I noticed a pretty young girl with dark hair coming towards us. I felt a sudden chill when I realized it was the same girl I had seen with Mr. Bartoli the other day. His eyes lit up as he saw her and he greeted her by kissing her on each cheek. I thought that now the day and news I had been dreading had finally come. Soon I would learn that he is in love with this young woman and will soon marry her. He turned to us in order to introduce her to us.

"I'd like you to meet my sister, Anna," Mr. Bartoli announced proudly.

His sister! I could hardly believe it. I was completely taken by surprise. Now that I was closer, I noticed that she *did* look remarkably like her mother. I was still left with the question of why Mr. Bartoli had not been honest with me.

Anna doesn't speak English but she greeted us with a charming smile. After speaking a little to Mr. Bartoli, she left to complete her errands. I think she was going to buy something at a shop nearby.

Mr. Bartoli explained that she would walk home from here, "It isn't that far ... there is a shortcut across the fields to our farm."

When no one else was near I said to him, "It was your sister I saw you with when I was returning from Mass. Why did you say it wasn't you that I had seen that day?" Now I was really acting too boldly.

"You said that you had seen me with a young woman. Anna's my sister. She's still a little girl, not a young woman," he answered simply. And for him the topic was closed.

I was surprised at this reasoning. Men certainly think differently than women. In any case, my mother would have said I had made a mountain out of a molehill, all for nothing!

When I woke this morning and looked out my window, there were grey veils of mist draped over the valley. We, on this high *monte*, were in the centre of the mist. I felt an unfathomable and, surely unreasonable, sadness in having to leave this place. The mist soon disappeared, and the sun edged its way through the remaining clouds. It was cooler and in the afternoon there were a few drops of rain. It was not a dreary rain; rather, it was refreshing; washing any remaining dust off trees and flowers and quenching their thirst. In fact, later the sun came out, even as it rained, and birds hopped around the garden in search of juicy worms.

Mr. Bartoli came and had me work on translating some passages from Dante. This was difficult for me, but

I worked away on it and did fairly well, I thought. To think that some people study Italian just to be able to read Dante's works in their original language! Dante was one of the first writers to write in the Italian of the people instead of Latin, somewhat like the English author, Chaucer.

The others had gone out into the garden, and although they were nearby, for a time Mr. Bartoli and I were alone.

When I was finished translating, Mr. Bartoli, looking very serious, told me to close my eyes and open my hands. I was a wary of doing this, wondering if, like my brother George when we were children, he would try and place a spider or something slimy in my hands. But Mr. Bartoli is an adult and my teacher; therefore, I couldn't truly expect such treachery. I did as he asked and he put something heavy and cold in my hands. When I opened my eyes, I saw a cameo brooch; a delicate carving of the Virgin Mary. It was beautiful; soft pink and cream circled with gold.

"This is for you," he said simply.

"But Mr. Bartoli, I cannot accept this. It would not be proper."

"Don't you like it?" he asked with surprise.

"I like it very much. I have never seen such a beautiful brooch!"

"Then please ... take it. To remember Italy. And me. You needn't tell anyone about it if you don't want to. You are good at keeping secrets," he smiled, and I knew he meant my going to Mass that afternoon, "I want to give it to you. It is a gift from your teacher to his student. Like the stained glass windows in cathedrals it will remind you of the Mother of Jesus and your visit to Montepulciano."

"Well, perhaps, ... I could keep it." I dreadfully wanted to have something that Mr. Bartoli had given me, but I was uncertain of the propriety of it.

"*Grazie, Chiara,*" and he took my fingers and closed them over the brooch.

"It is I who should say, *Grazie* to you, Mr. Bartoli and I do most sincerely say it."

"Now tell me that you will write to me from England."

"Of course, I shall if that is what you wish. But you must write to me first." I felt my heart would burst; I was so happy. I tried to be calm as I wrote my address on a page of my notebook and tore it out to give to him.

"Yes, I will write to you, and someday I hope to go to England again. Or you will come here and stay."

"Yes. I hope so, too," I answered softly and looked up into his face that by now was so dear to me.

"This is good-bye for now." As he stood up to leave, he said, *Arrivederci, Chiara.* Don't forget me and wait for me. I wanted to tell you this before, but it was best to wait until just before I leave." He took both my hands in his and kissed them and then he kissed me lightly on my forehead.

"I shall never forget you, and I will wait for you," I said, and I meant it with all my heart.

Chapter 9

Last night and again today, I took out my cameo to look at it several times. When I see it, I am able to believe what has happened in the last few days, for truly so much has happened in such a short time. Although we leave in a few days, I feel content and I am sure that Raffaele and I will be together again someday. Even now I can see his teasing, yet gentle, smile.

Mr. Fillmore and his mother went to Siena today because they weren't here when we had gone. Mr. Fillmore urged us to go again with them, but since Dorothea and I are leaving soon we really could not go. The others made their excuses as well. It is Good Friday (April 8) and they are certain to see some Good Friday Processions in Siena which would be interesting to see, but I'm not so certain Mr. Fillmore will appreciate them.

There was a procession in Montepulciano, too, even though I'm sure it was smaller than the one in Siena. Rev. Houghton, Dorothea, Miss Trent and I went to the *Piazza* at two in the afternoon when the procession was to begin. There were about fifty people already gathered when we arrived. The rain was falling drearily, as Don Angelo and an older priest, whom I did not know, organized the procession. When Don Angelo saw us, he asked us to join which we did.

I was surprised that Dorothea readily agreed. I think that she was curious to know what Papists did on Good Friday. Behind the priests and the altar boys, who accompanied them, were two young men who carried a large, plain wooden cross. It looked heavy. Down the streets and alleys we dutifully followed the cross. Many houses and shops had candles burning in their windows. We kept walking until we passed under the *Porto al Prato* and reached the Church of St. Agnes outside the town walls.

On entering the church, the two priests prostrated themselves in the centre aisle. They did this three times, each time closer to the altar. I couldn't help being both surprised and impressed with such an act of humility by those who are always looked on with awe by their flock. Some singing in Latin followed and Rev. Houghton explained that these verses were called "The Reproaches". He told us that in English they are:

My people, what have I done to you? How have I offended you? Answer me!

I led you out of Egypt; but you led your Saviour to the Cross.

For forty years I led you safely through the desert,

I fed you with manna from heaven and brought you to the land of plenty;

But you led your Saviour to the Cross.

O, My people! What have I done to you that you should testify against me?

Finally, everyone walked slowly to the front and took their turn to reverently kneel down and kiss the plain wooden cross. There was some singing as they did this. Because we are English and Protestant, we didn't take part, and I think no one expected us to. When we came out of the church it had stopped raining, and the sun was trying to shine through some ragged, leftover clouds. It was as if the weather was able to clear up now that the mournful procession had ended. We walked slowly back to the guesthouse without saying much. We were each deep in our own thoughts. Even Dorothea had nothing to say.

For the remainder of the day, I was content to look at my favorite view from the garden wall, although I did manage to do some packing as well.

When I was finished, I had some free time, so I looked through the book Mr. Fillmore had loaned me. I sat outside in the garden reading here and there so I could honestly say I had read it. Well, at least parts of it. My mind wandered and I was thinking of more pleasant things: my cameo brooch, the view of the valley and Mr. Bartoli, mostly of Mr. Bartoli ... my dear Raffaele, for surely now I can call him that. Was he already in Milan now, I wondered?

Mrs. Fillmore and her son returned late in the afternoon, and Mr. Fillmore came out to the garden. When he saw me he sat down on the bench beside me.

"I was hoping to find you here, Miss Ashford," he began.

"What did you think of Siena, Mr. Fillmore?" I asked him, trying to be congenial.

"Well, the city itself is interesting. But today being Good Friday, we encountered some of their Processions in Siena. It has only confirmed my idea of the wicked condition of the Roman Church."

I didn't really want to encourage him to give his ideas about the Roman Church, which I already had some idea of, and I realized since I had his book with me, I could conveniently change the subject and return the book to him.

"We are leaving Montepulciano in a few days, so please allow me to return your book. I was able to read a bit of it. I found it very ... inspiring." I was not being completely truthful again, but I hoped this was the kind of lie considered acceptable in order not to offend people.

"And now that you have read it, do you think you are called to be a missionary, Miss Ashford?"

"No, I don't believe so," I tried to sound thoughtful, "But I do thank you for your compliment."

"Well, I will continue to pray you will change your mind. Miss Ashford ... Claire, since I've met you I have come to the realization that God has brought me ..."

"Please, Mr. Fillmore ...," I did not want him to continue for I now guessed where it would lead.

"Miss Ashford, I feel God has led you to me. I am hoping you will accompany me to China ... as my wife."

I did not know how to answer him. This was my first proposal, after all, and now he seemed to want to make it impossible to refuse him, for it would also be refusing to obey God!

"I do not expect an answer now. I realize you have not known me long. But I do hope you will let me call on you in England, and then you can give me your answer."

"I fear the answer will not please you, sir."

"Please, pray about your answer. Ask God what His will is and obey Him."

The others had already gone in for dinner, and I was thankful to have an excuse to end the interview. We followed the others to the dining room.

My heart was heavy with this new dilemma. For truly, the only person I wanted to marry was Raffaele. But was that possible when we would soon be separated with a Continent between us? We didn't even know whether our parents would approve or when we would see each other again!

I have tried to put the conversation with Mr. Fillmore out of my mind, for I do not want to spoil my last few days in Montepulciano. I hope he will forget to visit me when he returns to England. Or that he will meet someone else on his travels. I will just have to deal with the problem when it arises again, but right now I will think of other things.

Tonight at midnight, when we were already in bed, the bells of all the churches in Montepulciano began to ring loudly announcing that "Christ had Risen". The Easter Vigil has ended.

Easter Sunday, April 10, 1898.   Rev. Houghton asked Mr. Fillmore to lead Morning Prayers this morning. Rev. Houghton's sermons are usually short, interesting and practical. Today Mr. Fillmore spoke for almost an hour; I'm sure Rev. Houghton could have said the same thing in half the time.   However, Rev. Houghton has had more experience, so I shouldn't judge Mr. Fillmore too harshly. He is indeed sincere, and I'm sure he put a lot of thought into his sermon. He spoke about "the fields white unto harvest" and how many people in the world are waiting to hear the Gospel. Was it partly to convince me of my missionary call I wonder? After all, it wasn't exactly a typical Easter sermon!

I felt myself wishing I could go to Mass again to celebrate the joy of the risen Christ in a proper Church instead of just the sitting room of the guesthouse.

For the rest of the day we talked or read. I suggested we go to the *Piazza* for the last time so Dorothea, Celia Trent and I went. This time we ordered our own *limonate*. I remembered the first day we had sat in the sunshine, and Raffaele, the "angel", had bought the drinks for us.

Easter Monday. Today we leave Montepulciano. Will I ever be back here again? In some ways it has seemed like home to me and, although I would certainly miss my family, I could happily stay here forever.

We said our farewells to everyone. Rev. Houghton seemed genuinely sorry to see us leave and wished us a safe and pleasant trip. He will be staying for another month. Miss Trent and the Pierces are staying in Italy a few more weeks and will travel to Rome and Sicily before sailing for England. Mrs. Fillmore and Mr. Fillmore will also be going to Sicily and then home.

Celia Trent and I have promised to visit each other when we get back to England and to keep in touch. I will miss her.

When we were about to leave, Mr. Fillmore took my hand and kissed it very formally and said good-bye by giving a flowery speech about missing the company of Miss Dorothea Weston and Miss Claire Ashford. I'm not sure why I always feel annoyed after he speaks; it is most unfair of me.

Chapter 10

I watched "the city set on a hill" disappear from view as our coach left Montepulciano. We are returning the same way we came; first to Livorno where we will board a packet that will take us across the Mediterranean to Marseilles. This will take us two to three days. Then we have to travel to the north of France and cross the channel to England. I hope it will not be a rough crossing this time.

Yesterday we passed by picturesque hill towns, which are similar to Montepulciano, and drove by fields where the grain is still a delicate green. Dorothea and I said little. I suppose we were each occupied with our own thoughts.

It was already late when we arrived in Livorno. Although it is not considered a particularly beautiful city, Livorno has been popular with the English for many years and is often called by its English name, Leghorn. I much prefer the Italian name; Leghorn sounds *most* unromantic and for some reason reminds me of chickens.

It seems one of the first Englishmen to come here was Sir Robert Dudley who arrived in 1605. He was the son of the Earl of Leicester (also named Robert Dudley), a favorite courtier of Queen Elizabeth. After landing in Italy, this second Dudley converted to Romanism. His motive was not particularly a spiritual one, as he had his first marriage annulled and married the English woman who had run away with him. For the remainder of his life, he built warships for the Grand Dukes in Livorno.

We won't be staying here long as we leave tomorrow. Now that we have left Tuscany, I am glad to be on my way home. Raffaele is in Milan anyway.

We boarded our packet without any problems and have started our voyage across the Mediterranean. It was a lovely sunny day, and the boat is full of returning English and French travelers. The boat is fairly crowded, and the meals are not as good as we had coming. Already I miss the good food we had in Italy, but I am looking forward to a typical English meal when we get home. We made some friends with an English couple from London and compared notes with them about our travels in Italy.

It is a few days since I have written. It is not easy to get a moment to write anything. We landed at Marseilles and are making our way to the north of France where we will cross the channel. I am looking forward to seeing my family, but I do miss Raffaele.

My fears have been realized, and again the Channel crossing has been rough. Thank goodness it is not a long journey, for I have not felt at all well. Naturally, I was very happy to see the sun shining on the white chalky cliffs at Dover as we approached England. After docking, we were able to secure a coach to take us directly to a hotel where we will stay until the morning. This will allow to us to go the entire way home in one day. I am certain I will feel better by morning now that I am on *terra ferma.*

April 16, 1898. Finally, we have arrived at Markham House. I was extremely tired, but as we neared home my excitement revived me. No doubt Dorothea felt the same, for she, too, seemed to regain energy as our journey came to an end.

I was so happy to see Mama and Papa and realized how much I had missed them. They thought I looked much healthier than when I had left. Everyone was happy with the gifts I had brought them. Beth and Margaret immediately put on their golden chains from the *Ponte Vecchio*. They kept asking questions about the places I had seen, the people I had met and what exciting things I had done. George is not home yet, but he is coming tomorrow. Elsa and Andrew came to welcome us back, and I had to hear about their latest wedding plans. That didn't bother me now, and I could truly wish them happy. I now realize that I was wrong and they are well-suited to each other. Both are a little lacking in sense.

My Mother announced that she had planned a lovely English meal for us ... roast chicken! Dorothea and I looked at each other and burst out laughing. We then had to explain that we had eaten roast chicken at the guest house almost every day, except for Fridays when we had fish. My mother promised to have a roast of beef the next evening.

After all the excitement, I went to bed in my own comfortable bed in my own room. How I had missed my familiar room! It did not seem so cold now. But I did not have the view of the valley, and the sunset which had become so familiar to me in Italy and I missed that a little.

Chapter 11

The weather was bright and warm today; almost as nice as Italy. Raffaele and Italy seem so distant; my experiences there are almost like a dream. But I look at my cameo brooch and know that some of it, at least, was real.

Dorothea finally enjoyed real English marmalade for breakfast. We talked about where we had gone, what we had eaten and the people we had met. We described our outings to Siena, Pienza, and Assisi and my family asked questions if we left out anything.

It is Sunday, and George had already arrived when we returned from the church service. He looked well and happy, and when I gave him his gifts he was pleased. I had to answer the same questions over again. Where had we gone? What had we done? Whom had we met? What did I like best? What was my favorite place? He hopes to go with some friends soon and wanted to know which sights I thought were most interesting. He was disappointed that we had not gone to Venice and Rome because he has heard these cities are not to be missed.

I had not told anyone about Raffaele, but when George and I were alone later today, I told him about my tutor and our friendship. He guessed my true feelings and as a concerned older brother questioned me about Raffaele's character.

"What do you know really about him, Claire? You have only known him for a short time, and he is a foreigner, someone who thinks very differently than we do."

"In Italy, I was the foreigner," I argued.

"All right ... you know what I mean. He is a foreigner to us ... to your family."

He sounded a bit like Dorothea, but I know it was from a different motive. He is not narrow- minded; George could never be that, but he was worried about his younger sister giving her heart to a stranger too easily.

"I know men, and they can be quite ruthless when it comes to women," George said seriously.

"And you? Are you also ruthless with women?" I teased.

"No. Well, not always," he laughed.

"Then it is not *all* men that are "ruthless", just some," I argued.

"Well, do be careful, Claire. This Italian fellow is miles away and lives in a different world than we do. For one thing, he is a Romanist."

"I haven't married him yet, George. And please don't mention anything to Mama or Papa or anyone else. There is no need. Promise?"

"Yes, I promise ... but please talk to me before you do anything rash."

I didn't tell George about the cameo nor about my sympathies for the Romanists which, I guessed, would truly shock him.

It is over a week since I have written to you, my diary. Today I had to write and tell you that when I went down stairs this morning, I noticed a letter on the hall table. It was addressed to me and had been stamped in Italy! I hurried back to my room and excitedly tore open that precious envelope.

Yes, Raffaele has written from Milan (or *Milano*, as he wrote).

(And here James found a yellowed paper folded into the pages of the diary.)

Ma bella Chiara;

Yes, it is me, your tutor, Raffaele, writing to you from Milano. I am staying near the university with some friends, also from Toscano and also in the Catholic Youth group I told you about. I have made some new friends, too, one from Genoa (Giorgio) and another from Torino (Antonio). They very much think like I do, and we are busy seeing the sights of Milano when we are not studying or helping the poor and the sick. We are able to visit them and bring food and medicine. Sometimes we go on marches; when we know there will be government officials there. We want the government to do more for those who do not have work and are unable to support their families.

Yesterday, I went with my new friends to Santa Maria della Grazie. *It is a Dominican convent and in the refectory there is a painting in* tempera *on the end wall. This painting is very famous, so I'm sure you have heard of it:* L'Ultima Cena *or in English, The Last Supper. The artist, Leonardo da Vinci, was commissioned by his sponsor to paint it in 1495. The painting is of Jesus and His twelve Apostles eating the Passover meal together, and it captures the time when Jesus instituted the Eucharist. Leonardo has painted the moment when the Apostles were told that someone would betray Him. They all wonder who is the one who will betray their Master, and shock is shown on their faces. It is a magnificent painting, and I am sorry you did not see it when you were in Italy. When you come again, I will take you to see it.*

We go to the Duomo for Mass every day. It is much nicer than the unfinished one in Montepulciano! It is baroque in style and I think you would like it. You would also like La Madonnina *(The Little Madonna), the golden statue of the Virgin Mary which is on top of the Duomo. She has been there since 1774 and stands with her arms open wide, welcoming everyone to the great city of Milano.*

When our classes are finished, we often go to the Galleria – *the full name is* Galleria Vittoriao Emmanuele II, *named after our King. Do you remember I told you about him? The* Galleria *was finished in 1867, and the ceiling is made of iron and glass. It is so modern it even has electric lights! We can sit and enjoy our coffee or wine and watch the people go by. In fact, it is called* il solleto di Milano *as the* Milanesi *treat it as their sitting room. There are many interesting people in this city to watch!*

I have some excellent professors; although some are comical. They rush around in their rumpled gowns and hats looking like lost blackbirds. But I must not criticize. I enjoy the classes very much and several of our professors are brilliant. I admit that there are some lectures which are boring, and these we escape whenever we can.

I especially like one professor (Professor Tadeschi) who lectures us in Philosophy. To learn about Aristotle – it is just fascinating! You may think that it has nothing to do with the problems of today but there you would be mistaken. It has to do with the problems of every age.

I hope your trip back to England was enjoyable and not too tiring. Now you are with your famiglia, *and you will forget about your tutor here in Italy. But I remember your promise not to forget me.*

I very much miss you. I pray to our Blessed Mother that you will be able to return soon or that I can go to England.

> *Con 'amor,*
> *Raffaele*

No one else knew I had received the letter. I immediately took out a pen and some of the marbled paper I had brought back from Italy for myself and began to write an answer. I told him of our trip back to England, being with my family again and how everyone liked the gifts I had brought them. I will also tell him how much I miss him. It will take me several days to answer his letter.

Dorothea returned to her home today and life is more or less back to normal.

Saturday, April 23, 1898. Today Elsa and Andrew were married in our parish church. It was a lovely wedding; the weather couldn't have been better. It was so pleasant that we were able to have the reception outside in the church garden. Lilacs and peonies were in full bloom, and Elsa, her golden hair swept up in fetching curls, looked pretty as all brides do. Her gown was pure white satin and lace and it suited her very well. Since Queen Victoria was married in a white gown it has become quite the fashion. I think it is a lovely idea. I was one of the bridesmaids, but I hope it won't be too long before I am the bride! I must say that today I missed Raffaele more than ever, as Elsa and Andrew are so happy together. I would like others to see that I, too, have someone who loves me. Funny how I used to think Andrew was handsome. He doesn't seem especially handsome to me now. I suppose there are those who would not call Raffaele in any way outstanding, but how nice he looks to me! How much has changed in just a few months. And how much I have changed!

Chapter 12

Monday, April 25, 1898. This morning I was in my room finishing my letter to Raffaele when Beth and Margaret burst into my room.

"Claire ... there is a gentleman to see you. Mother says you must come to the drawing room right away."

I must say that my heart gave a sudden expectant start ... but no, I knew it couldn't be Raffaele. Surely he wouldn't be able to come yet, and I was certain he would have sent word before he came.

I gave a quick glance in the mirror, straightened my hair, smoothed the front of my dress and went down the stairs as quickly as I could.

On entering the drawing room, I saw that my mother and father were entertaining a gentleman whose back was turned towards me. When I entered my mother looked up and saw me.

"Claire, Mr. Fillmore has been telling us about meeting you in Italy."

Mr. Fillmore! I had forgotten about him and his promise, or threat, to visit me when he returned to England. He turned, took my hand and kissed it.

"It's wonderful to see you again, Miss Ashford. I've been making the acquaintance of your parents and telling them something of our experiences in Montepulciano." Our experiences!

"How nice of you to call, Mr. Fillmore. I trust your mother is well?" I managed to say, still being somewhat taken aback at his unexpected arrival. I hoped my voice did not betray the shock or the displeasure I felt.

"She is fine, thank you. She sends you her greetings and would have come with me today, but she is still weary after our long journey home. We loved Sicily, but Naples was too dirty and crowded for her sensitive nature. It's a pity, though, you couldn't have seen Sicily and its Greek temples."

We talked for awhile in the drawing room, and then father suggested that Mr. Fillmore might like to see our garden. I suppose my parents were impressed with Mr. Fillmore who had the air of an educated and well-to-do English gentleman. Were they hoping that here was a match for their eldest daughter? They probably had guessed his interest in me but did not know he had already asked me to accompany him to China as a missionary. What would they have thought of that, I wondered, as Mr. Fillmore and I walked out into the garden? Would they approve, or would they be horrified to see me go so far away to a strange land?

We walked past the lovely oak trees towards an old wrought iron bench we kept near the end of our garden, and Mr. Fillmore commented that we had a lovely home. I didn't know what to say, so I remained silent. Uncharacteristically, after that, so was Mr. Fillmore. We sat down, and after more silence, he asked me if I had thought over the proposal that he had made the last time we spoke.

"Mr. Fillmore," I began and knew not how to continue, "I am most honoured by your proposal, but I'm afraid my affections are engaged elsewhere. I should have mentioned this to you when you first spoke to me, but I was not sure about the feelings of the gentleman then." Inwardly I was thinking that even if I did not love someone else, I could not marry Mr. Fillmore. I would rather not marry at all than be with someone I did not love and could never love.

"I see," he answered, "This gentleman ... does he live nearby?"

"I'm afraid I'm not at liberty to say," I answered awkwardly. It was a rather strange thing for a lady to say in such a situation.

"I see," he repeated. I think he didn't believe me. He had not expected a refusal.

"I am sorry ... but I know I wouldn't make a good missionary either."

"I think you are quite wrong about that. You have all the qualities to be a great missionary."

"Perhaps you have imagined these qualities, sir."

We walked back to the house; we had nothing more to say to each other. My mother invited him to stay for a cup of tea, and to be polite he did stay. Then he thanked us for a lovely afternoon and left. I felt that his heart had not been broken but his feelings had been injured. I think I would have felt worse if I had felt he truly loved me.

"Mr. Fillmore seems like such a nice gentleman," my mother said, and my father nodded in agreement, "I do hope he calls again."

Oh Father, please don't wish that, I thought! Parents are always hopeful that their daughters will find someone suitable to marry, I suppose.

Tuesday, April 26, 1898. This morning I finished my letter to Raffaele and took it myself it to the postal office to have it franked.

Then in the afternoon, mother and I visited a family in our parish. The wife has pleurisy, the husband is out of work and there are five children to care for. We took some medicine and food. I suppose this is a type of missionary work, too. Or does one have to go to a foreign country to be a missionary?

Today, May 5, 1898, my mother received a surprising letter from Dorothea. She is to marry Mr. Fillmore! Shortly after his visit here he must have gone to see Dorothea. She sounds very happy and said that even when she was in Italy she felt that he was interested in her! Of course, she doesn't know, and I hope will never find out, that he had asked me to marry him only a few weeks ago. She is overjoyed to be going to China as a missionary, too, although she knows she will face many hardships. They are to be married at Christmas and will leave for China sometime in the New Year. What a surprise ... and relief!

My mother was extremely surprised, "I must admit I thought he was interested in you. He looked at you very fondly and came all this way to see you. Why would he do that if he were planning on asking Dorothea to marry him?"

"Mother," I began somewhat fearfully, "Mr. Fillmore did ask me to marry him when we were still in Italy. He came here to find out my answer."

"You said, 'No'?" she asked incredulously.

"Yes, I do not love him," I answered simply.

"Love? Do you think that you have the luxury of loving whomever you marry?"

"But you loved Father when you married him, didn't you?"

"No, not when I agreed to marry him. I hardly knew him then. But love grew, and after a year or so of marriage, I had grown to love him. I'm sure Mr. Fillmore is very kind, and you would have come to love him in time."

"And you and Father would not have minded me going to China?"

"Oh, that would have been dreadful, Claire. For this, I'm glad you refused Mr. Fillmore."

"Surely if I were to have married Mr. Fillmore, I should have had some desire to help him in his work in China."

"Yes, I suppose so. And come to think of it, it didn't take long for him to fall out of love with you," my mother wryly observed.

"Yes. It seems that God was wrong about me being His chosen wife for Mr. Fillmore, too," I added with a laugh, "To be truthful I think he just wanted to find a wife, any wife, before going so far away from England."

"My daughter is much wiser than she was last year," my mother looked at me and smiled

"I do hope they will be happy. You mustn't say a word to anyone about this, even Father."

"I promise," she answered.

It seems to me that some men look for a wife in much the same as they look for new shoes. So much for love! But I know that love can be real; although I believe it is rarer than I previously thought.

I was relieved that we would not have to have any more visits from Mr. Fillmore, at least as a bachelor. Furthermore, I am happy for Dorothea who, although she is several years older than Mr. Fillmore, will make a faithful missionary and a suitable companion for him. I did not think it was the right time to tell Mother about Raffaele.

Chapter 13

It has been many days since I've written in you, my diary, and it is already June. How much can change in just one day! The twentieth of May began as any usual day with the morning sun already shining brightly into my bedroom when I awoke. I had no idea that my life would be changed forever by that day. I was in the garden reading when Nora came to get me.

"Miss Claire, a gentleman has come to call on you. Your father is with him in the drawing room."

"Thank you, Nora. Do you know who it is?"

"No, I don't Miss. I was just told to find you and ask you to go to the drawing room."

Another gentleman caller! My first thought was that Mr. Fillmore had returned for some reason, and I admit that I felt a little annoyed. When I entered the room, I was very glad to see my old friend, Rev. Houghton!

"Rev. Houghton, how nice to see you. I'm so glad you've come. I see you've met my father. Rev. Houghton is a very dear friend that Dorothea and I met in Italy, Father."

Rev. Houghton took my hand and kissed it.

"My dear Miss Ashford, it is good to see you again. But I'm afraid I come with some tragic news, and you will not be happy to see me after you've heard it."

Rev. Houghton looked very serious and so did Father.

"I regret to have to tell you this ... before I left Italy we had news that Mr. Bartoli had ... died in Milan."

Mr. Bartoli had died? What did he mean? I had just had a letter from him. I felt faint and dizzy; all of a sudden it seemed as if I could not breathe. Seeing my distress, someone brought me a glass of water.

"How .... how did it happen? Do you know? Was he ill?"

"No. No one is sure exactly what happened, but these are dangerous times in parts of Italy. He was with a Catholic Youth Group that supported the Pope, and on May 7 there was a protest in Milan. A group of poor people was asking the government for work and food for their families. It is not certain if Mr. Bartoli and others were there with the group, or if they just happened to be there at the wrong time. The protesters were not armed, but the army was ordered to fire at them anyway. Over 300 people were killed and many more were injured."

My mother came in, and she was told the news. Rev. Houghton explained that Mr. Bartoli had been my tutor in Montepulciano.

"Well, as Rev. Houghton said, these are dangerous times in Italy. Things are bound to happen," my father said.

"I'm ever so glad that you are safely at home. Thank God you are not wandering around in foreign countries." My mother may have been thinking how thankful she was I would not be going to China. She could not have guessed that this "tutor" was the man I had hoped to marry and that I had seriously thought of living in "a foreign country" to be with him. I was certain Rev. Houghton did know my feelings. I think he had guessed even when we were in Montepulciano.

I wanted to weep, but tears would not come. I could not really believe that this had happened. It must be a mistake. It was all a mistake....yes; it was someone else and not

Raffaele who had died. Someone would soon send news that it had all been a mistake.

Rev. Houghton handed me a small ivory envelope, "Mr. Bartoli's sister asked me to give this to you."

I opened it and read it. I understood the Italian, but the words still did not seem to be true. Anna, Raffaele's sister, confirmed what Rev. Houghton had told us.

After that, I do not remember what happened. When I woke up in my bed, I felt feverish, confused and so very thirsty.

My mother was sitting by my bed, and when I opened my eyes she called my father. They gave me some tea, and the warm liquid felt good to my parched throat.

"You must eat something, Claire," my mother urged offering me some broth.

I shook my head. I could not eat.

"Where is Rev. Houghton?" I asked.

"He has gone to stay with friends nearby. He said he would call tomorrow to see how you are."

I think Rev. Houghton had explained to my parents that Mr. Bartoli had been more to me than just a tutor. He had also passed on his good opinion of him to my parents.

After being ill for several weeks, I am now feeling somewhat better. I am able to eat and have been sitting outside in the warm sunshine. My strength is gradually returning, but things will never be the same.

I imagine what it must have been like for the Bartoli family when they heard that terrible news. I have forced myself to think of it for then I may be able to accept that this tragedy has indeed happened. In my mind, I picture the notice of Raffaele's death, edged in black, and posted on the building where we had seen the death notices. And then a procession; a young boy wearing a white lace surplice, carrying a crucifix. A priest, perhaps Don Angelo, leading

Raffaele's family and friends and finally the coffin through winding streets. I see huge wreaths of flowers placed around the altar of the *Duomo*. And I imagine the sombre music and the mourners walking from the faceless *Duomo* down to the cemetery with spear-like cypresses guarding the road. I see the *Chiesa Madonna di San Bagio* nearby. I imagine all this, and yet I still hope it has been a mistake. How could someone so good die in this terrible way? Why had God allowed this to happen?

Rev. Houghton has come several times to visit before returning home to Oxford. I had many talks with him especially about our time in Montepulciano. And yes, I did share my feelings for Raffaele with Rev. Houghton and showed him the cameo that Raffaelle had given to me. I asked him why God would answer my prayers and then cruelly take Raffaele. He answered that he did not know, but we must believe that God always does what is just and right. The act of killing those people was done by men; they were not doing God's will but their own. Unfortunately, it is human beings who kill each other.

He gave me a small card engraved with the words of a hymn written by Cardinal Newman while he was still a vicar of the Church of England, "Lead, Kindly Light". It is a lovely poem and brought me some small comfort.

My parents realize what Mr. Bartoli had meant to me and the understanding we had. They did wonder about Raffaele's character and why he had put himself in such a dangerous situation. I explained to Mother and Father that Raffaele's father is a landowner and that some people oppose landowners because they are rich and powerful. Unfortunately, there are landowners who do not treat their workers well. There are also those who do not want the Church to have too much power. Rev. Houghton had told us that there were many people killed that day; some may have just been there to protest along with the poor. None of the protesters had been armed. Raffaele may even have been there quite by accident. However, knowing his desire to help the poor and from what he had said in his letter, I believe he had gone with a purpose. He was that kind of person, and that was one of the reasons he had gone to Milan. Rev. Houghton's defence of Raffaele's character had done much to influence my parents in his favour. I did not tell Mother and Father about the cameo brooch ... that will remain my secret.

George came soon after he heard the news.

"I'm sorry this happened, Claire. We don't always know the reasons these things take place." Thankfully he did not say, "Perhaps it was all for the best."

I still want to join the Roman Church but I have to be certain that my interest in it is not just because of Raffaele. If I had married him, I would have naturally joined his Church. But now ... I do not have to leave the Church of England. Do I really want to? And what are my reasons? Are they just romantic notions that I acquired in Italy? I am not always sure I believe the doctrines I will have to accept in order to become a Romanist. Is the view of the Virgin Mary in the Church of England that different from that of the Romanists? Yet, I still long to go to Mass again; I am not sure why.

I will never be reconciled to the loss of so great a friend and the first person I ever really loved. But I do think that Raffaele would not want me to mourn him forever. He would want me to be happy someday ... happy that I had known him. I remembered what he had said once, "We can choose to be cheerful or not, even if life is difficult. Why not choose to laugh and sing when we can?" I may never marry and I certainly do not feel like laughing or singing yet, but I know that once I was loved and that I loved. That is enough for me now.

What happens from now on will happen to a different Claire Ashford, for the old one has died.

∾

Tucked into this page was a small envelope, a folded newspaper clipping and a gold-edged ivory card.

James opened the envelope and read the note that Raphael's sister, Anna Bartoli had written to Claire.

Gentilissima signorina Ashford;

Mi dispiace trasmettere le notizie di Raffaele, il mio caro fratello ed il vostro amico è morto. È stato sparato a Milano, il 7 di Maggio. Non sappiamo se fosse perché era il figlio di un proprietario o perché era apparteneve alla Societa della Gioventu Cattolica Italiana o se fosse un incidente. Preghi per noi, la sua famiglia, che lo amavamo molto.

I send to you with Signore Houghton.

Sua amica, Anna Bartoli

An English translation was written in Claire's handwriting:

I regret to tell you that Raffaele Bartoli, my dear brother and your friend, is dead. He was shot in Milan on the 7th of May. We don't know why he was there. Perhaps he just happened to be there, but we think he was there to support the poor as he was a member of the Young Italian Catholics. Pray for us, his family, who loved him very much. I am sending this with Rev. Houghton. Your friend, Anna Bartoli

The newspaper clipping was from a British paper, dated July 30, 1900, so it had appeared in the paper several years after Raffaele had died. It read:

Italian Monarch Assassinated
July 30, 1900.

King Humbert (Umberto) I of Italy was fatally shot in Monza, a city north of Milan, yesterday. The assassin, Gaetano Bresca, has been arrested by Italian police. Bresca is originally from the town of Coiano, near Prato, in Tuscany. He emigrated to Paterson, New Jersey in the United States, where he worked as a weaver in a silk factory. Mr. Bresca was also involved in the publishing of an anarchist Italian-language newspaper, La Questione Sociale. *It is thought that he shot King Umberto in order to avenge the Bava-Baccaris Massacre in Milan, May 7, 1898 in which 350 unarmed demonstrators were killed by the army. Mr. Bresca's sister was one of those that died in the massacre ordered by General Fiorenzo Bava-Baccaris.*

The funeral for King Humbert will be held in Rome and he will be buried in the Pantheon. He is survived by his wife, Queen Margherita, who is greatly loved by the Italian people, and their son, now King Victor Emmanuel III.

There was a photo of King Umberto I in full military uniform in the article, and the section about the massacre in Milan had been underlined by someone.

The last item, the ivory card, edged in gold, was engraved with the following poem:

> *Lead, Kindly Light, amid the encircling gloom,*
> *Lead Thou me on!*
> *The night is dark, and I am far from home-*
> *Lead Thou me on!*
> *Keep Thou my feet; I do not ask to see*
> *The distant scene, – one step enough for me.*
>
> *I was not ever thus, nor prayed that Thou*
> *Shouldst lead me on.*

I loved to choose and see my path; but now
Lead Thou me on!
I loved the garish day, and, spite of fears,
Pride ruled my will: remember not past years.

So long Thy power hath blest me, sure it still
Will lead me on,
O'er moor and fen, o'er crag and torrent, till
The night is gone;
And with the morn those angel faces smile
Which I have loved long since, and lost awhile.

John Henry Newman, 1833

Chapter 14

In the morning after breakfast, James decided he would call Mr. Winston to tell him about the diary and his progress in finding the owner of the cameo.

"Winston? This is James Marsh. I wanted to let you know that I've found the owner of the cameo."

"Indeed? Are you certain?" He sounded somewhat disappointed.

"Well, reasonably so. A short time ago, I was contacted by the granddaughter of a woman who once lived at Markham House. The grandmother had received a gift of a cameo brooch while visiting Italy about fifty years ago. I've been reading the grandmother's diary, and in it she accurately describes our cameo brooch."

"I'm afraid I'm not free today to meet you, but we could get together tomorrow for lunch. If you are free then, of course. At "The Catherine Wheel"? I think you know it ... it's near our office. You can give me the details then."

"Yes, I know the place. I can be there by noon."

That evening James settled in his chair with the usual brandy to finish reading the few remaining pages of the diary.

∾

Saturday, May 13, 1899. It has been over a year since I was in Italy, and I have not written in you, my diary, for some time. Memories of my time there seem more distant, but I still think of those days when I was so happy. Rev. Houghton has been to visit me often over the past months. He has been a true friend.

On one of his visits, I told Rev. Houghton about Dorothea and Mr. Fillmore's engagement. He was surprised but agreed that she will make an excellent missionary wife. He remarked that they had a lot in common especially their shared evangelical outlook.

"And a lack of sympathy for 'Romanists'," I added, somewhat uncharitably.

Rev. Houghton laughed at that and admitted he had to agree.

Rev. Houghton told me that he has definitely decided to leave the Church of England and join the Church of Rome. It is an important decision for him as he will have to leave his livelihood, as well. He confided to me that he has hopes of securing a teaching position in a boy's school nearby which is under the direction of a Catholic Order.

"You have come to terms with the idea of having a Pope, then?" I asked, remembering his comment that evening in Montepulciano.

"I have been reading about the office of the Pope and how Our Lord gave St. Peter the keys to the kingdom of heaven. It seems to be related to the office of the Prime Minister mentioned by the prophet, Isaiah. I see that the office is indeed necessary. God appointed leaders throughout history ... Abraham, Moses and others," he explained, "We need a leader, under the Holy Spirit, to guide the Church. There are always matters about morality that need decisions; some modern temptations are not mentioned in Scripture. If there is no leader, denominations will go on multiplying as people run off to start new churches that fit with their own ideas."

"But haven't there been Popes who weren't good men? How can such men be infallible?"

"To be infallible does not mean *sinless*. Popes are only human, just as the writers of Scripture were. But the Holy Spirit guided Matthew, Luke, Paul and others to write Holy Scripture. It is the office of the Pope that is infallible because, whoever he is, he is guided by the Holy Spirit when making decisions about doctrine or morality. Jesus promised to be with the Church until the end of the world and I believe this is the way He keeps his promise."

I admitted that I, too, had been thinking of becoming a Romanist even though I still have many questions.

"I have spoken to the priest in this parish, but he said that I should not do anything yet. He advised me to pray and wait for awhile. He said that people sometimes make hasty decisions when they have lost someone ... they love."

"He gave you wise advice. You may have felt drawn to the Roman Church because of Mr. Bartoli. But I'm sure God will guide you."

Today I was pleasantly surprised by a visit from Celia Trent. We had a lovely afternoon and reminisced about our time in Montepulciano. She was ill after returning from Italy and was sorry that she was unable to visit me sooner. Rev. Houghton has kept in touch with her aunt and uncle, and she heard about Raffaele's death from them.

"I knew you had special feelings for Mr. Bartoli," she said, "Every time he looked at you, you blushed."

"That wouldn't necessarily mean I was in love with him," I said in my own defence, "I have always blushed at the slightest provocation."

She had not heard, though, that Dorothea and Mr. Fillmore were engaged to be married.

"That *is* a surprise! I thought that it was you he that he fancied when we were in Italy," she said innocently.

"And at first, I thought it was you he liked!" I exclaimed, "Actually, he did express some interest in me before we left, but because of my feelings for Raffaele, I tried to discourage him." I did not speak of his coming here since my arriving home and his offer of marriage to me. As much as I wanted to share this with her, I did not feel it would be fair to Dorothea.

"Oh, I don't think he would have suited you at all. He would be much too dull," she laughed.

I told her of my desire to join the Romanist church, and she was astonished at this.

"Why ever would you want to leave the church of your childhood? I feel quite satisfied with it. It is, after all, English and so it suits me. Is it because of your attachment to Mr. Bartoli, do you think?"

"At first, I think it was a romantic idea for me ... certainly connected with my feelings for Raffaele."

"I can see that you would feel that then, but now ... are you still thinking of leaving the Church of England?"

"Yes. Now it is not just a whim or a necessity because of marriage. I have been reading a lot ... the tracts of Cardinal Newman and some writings of the Church Fathers that Rev. Houghton has loaned me. I can see that having a Pope is a reasonable idea, believe it or not, and I think the Catholic Church has been much misrepresented to us. I do love the prayers in our Prayer Book, and I would never have imagined that one day I would join the Papists and their Latin prayers. But I feel mysteriously drawn to the Roman Church. It's like a magnet ... and yet I still hesitate to leave what is familiar."

"Well, you must be very careful and find out for certain what they believe. One can be so misled nowadays."

"Rev. Houghton is joining the Romanists. Do you think he would be misled easily?"

"No, he has studied theology and is a sensible man, to be sure. He would have to leave his position as Vicar though, wouldn't he?" she asked.

"Yes, he has said he plans to procure a teaching position somewhere. And what about you, Celia? Has anyone managed to win your heart? The man who does is truly fortunate," I said changing the subject.

"Not yet," she smiled, "But I am content to wait for the right one."

It was a lovely visit, and she promised to come again.

Another surprise today (Saturday, May 20, 1899) as Dorothea came. She, too, apologised for not coming sooner but said she has been very busy preparing for her wedding and journey to China. To me she has changed, and I think it is her engagement and impending marriage that has caused this change. She is more attractive now and appears more confident. Is it knowing that one is loved that makes a woman more beautiful? Or is it being truly happy?

At first, Dorothea barely mentioned Raffaele or the tragedy of his death and talked mostly of her own plans.

Then she began, "I am surprised that you had considered marrying Mr. Bartoli, Claire. You would have had to join his Church, and you would have had to live in Italy. It would have been very difficult for you. To be sure, he seemed very nice, but one can never really tell what they are like."

"Would living in Italy be more difficult than living in China, as you will be doing? I have never been to China, but I think it is much different from England, whereas Italy has more in common with England."

"Well, I will be taking the message of Christianity to China. You would have joined with the Romanists and would have not been evangelizing them."

"Do you not think that Roman Catholics are Christians then?" I asked, surprised.

"No. In the middle ages, the Romanists departed from Christian belief. That is when all this "popery" began and they forgot the true message of the Bible."

"But it seems to me we wouldn't even have the Bible if the Catholic monks of the Middle Ages hadn't made copies of it and preserved it over the centuries."

Just then Mother came in, and tea was served, so I was rescued from any further discussion. I cannot explain why I feel so attracted to the Church that she is convinced is the "whore of Babylon".

When Mother was there, the conversation turned to other topics.

I am glad that Dorothea is happy to be marrying Mr. Fillmore and content with her future as a missionary; for I truly believe she has a good heart and a desire to serve God. How sad it is, though, that her mind is so closed to what the early Christians believed without having read what the Church Fathers say.

Today (Monday, May 22, 1899) Rev. Houghton came. I asked him more questions about the Church and the book he had loaned to me, Cardinal Newman's autobiography, *Apologia pro Sua*.

Then without warning, he changed the subject, "We have become good friends, you and I, have we not?"

"Rev. Houghton, you know I value your friendship a great deal. You have helped me through an extremely difficult time."

"Claire, I realize you think of me as much older than you, but I feel we do have a lot in common. And I have become very fond of you ... I want to shield you from any more unhappiness. What I am trying to say and not doing it very well, is that I love you. Even someone my age can fall in love, you know. Would you ever consent to be my wife?"

I must admit, Rev. Houghton's sudden proposal was most unexpected! Although I knew he was fond of me, I imagined he thought of me more as a daughter than a wife, and I have thought of him as a spiritual advisor. It is true he is older than I, and he has been so very kind to me. He is a good person and we do share many interests. Even in Montepulciano, I respected him and his opinions a great deal, and now I have truly become fond of him.

"I wonder if someday you could grow to love me, too," he said and with that the subject was closed for the time, for I was hesitant to say more, and he seemed to feel he had said too much already.

When he had gone, I thought about what he had said. Could I love him someday? Would I be happy if I married him? He certainly didn't fit the picture of the man I had hoped to marry; young, handsome and not too serious. He is different from Raffaele, even though Raffaele could be serious at times, too. It is true that Rev. Houghton is intelligent, wise and dependable. Are these qualities are more important in a husband than the ones I have considered up till now?

Again my life seems to be at a crossroad and I have to decide which direction I should take. Life has so many choices.

Today (Thursday, May 25, 1899) when Rev. Houghton came, he asked me if I had thought about his proposal. Did I think I would ever being able to love him?

"Rev. Houghton, indeed I have been thinking about what you said the last time you were here. I thank you for all your kindness and understanding in the past weeks. I do love you as a friend, and yes, I could learn to love you as you love me."

"Then you consent to be my wife?"

"Yes," I answered simply and without hesitation.

He smiled and said, "Then, my dear, if we are to be engaged, I think you should call me Edward."

There are many kinds of love. My love for Edward will never be the same as my love for Raffaele, but it will be just as real.

Sunday, June 18, 1899. Today Edward joined the Roman Catholic Church. We continue to have many discussions about this, and when I have a question about doctrine, he patiently explains it to me. We plan to be married next year, and I will join the Church sometime before that. He has already taken a position as a tutor at a Grammar school close to Oxford. There is a small but adequate flat in the school where we will live.

And Celia Trent has consented to be my bridesmaid! My brother, George, was here when she was visiting recently. They seemed to get on well, and I can't help hoping they might form an attachment. He could find no other person as sweet and sensible as she is. I would certainly be very happy to have her as a sister-in-law.

Although my parents like Edward immensely, they do not understand why he felt it necessary to leave the Church of England and join the Roman Church. They were even more surprised that I had also been thinking of doing that very thing, even before Edward asked me to marry him. My father blames himself for sending me to Italy thus putting me under the spell of the Papists. It has been difficult for them, but they have finally accepted this state of affairs. Even though things have changed, I'm sure we will always be welcome to visit at my parents' home.

❧

James closed the brown leather diary. He had come to the end of Claire Ashford's story. What a surprise that she had married Rev. Houghton! He would never have guessed that ending. He wondered if George and Celia Trent did marry. He must ask Claire Bromley the next time he sees her.

Chapter 15

J ames made his way into town early the next morning. He felt a sense of accomplishment, however small, at finding the owner of the cameo. Clare Ashford's diary was in his briefcase, and he hurried to "The Catherine Wheel", one of the many old inns in this part of England named after St. Catherine of Alexandria and the instrument of her torture.

Mr. Winston arrived a few minutes late and was cheerful in spite of the impending loss of the cameo. Had he decided it was not worth all the trouble, after all?

"Well now, James what's the story of the brooch?" Mr. Winston asked after they had been seated comfortably and had ordered.

"About a month after I saw you last, a Miss Bromley answered an ad I put in the paper. She told me that her grandmother had been given a cameo brooch while visiting Italy in 1898. Markham House had been her family home at that time. Miss Bromley had a diary which her grandmother kept when she was in Italy. I've read it, and here ...," James turned to the page in the diary and showed it to Winston, "... she tells of receiving a cameo with a carving of the Virgin."

Mr. Winston read the page quickly as he sipped his ale, "Well, I suppose it would be too much of a coincidence not to be hers. The grandmother is still alive?"

"No. She died several years ago, but her daughter is. So far, I've only met the granddaughter ... she lives with an aunt in Littlemore."

"Good work, Captain Marsh. When I get back to the office, I'll call Mr. Spence and ask him what he advises and then I'll contact you. For now, let's just enjoy our lunch. Now what have you been doing?"

Mr. Winston wasn't giving up the cameo that easily, after all. And now he insisted on acting chummy.

"To tell you the truth, I've spent a lot of time reading the diary ... I read the entire thing."

"Surely that wasn't necessary."

"No, but it turned out to be a damned interesting story ... a lot of Italian history I wasn't aware of."

"Are you interested in Italian history? You weren't in Italy during the war were you?"

"No, I was in Asia. But I am interested in European history. I hope that in destroying fascism, we haven't also destroyed the great art in the cathedrals and galleries of Italy. They are part of the heritage of all Europe."

Soon their orders of mixed grill and chips came, and although James usually found pub food too greasy and heavy, he was hungry and managed to eat almost all of it.

The rest of the time they talked about the topics of the day; the trials of the war criminals in Nuremburg and closer to home, the Labour Government's plan to institute a National Health Service. The time went by quickly, and James had to admit he enjoyed the visit. Possibly he had judged Winston too harshly before. As he was leaving, Winston reminded James he would call him regarding the cameo.

The following day James started to catch up with correspondence he had neglected, and he forgot about the cameo. Then in the late afternoon, the phone rang. It was Mr. Winston.

"Captain Marsh, Spence has looked into the matter of the cameo. He has substantiated some of the facts mentioned in the diary, so he thinks the woman who contacted you has a valid claim on the brooch. If we proceeded with a court case, we'd spend a lot of unnecessary time and money. Would you be able to pick up the brooch sometime when you're in town and turn it over to the woman? Or would you rather I have it delivered to her?"

"Oh, I'd be happy to pick it up and see that Miss Bromley gets the cameo," James answered.

After several days, James had to go into town for something and called in at Mr. Winston's office to pick up the cameo. He was anxious to tell Miss Bromley that the cameo was hers, or at least, her mother's. He hadn't called her when Mr. Winston had first contacted him, so he decided to call her straightaway that afternoon.

Claire Bromley answered the phone, and James thought she sounded pleased to hear from him. She was looking forward to finally being able to see the cameo and telling her mother about it. As this Saturday was her day off, she asked if James were free to visit her mother then. That way he could give her mother the cameo himself. He thought it would be interesting to meet Claire's mother, and find out more about the grandmother's story, so he readily agreed. He was rather looking forward to seeing Claire Bromley again, too.

That morning it was cloudy but at least not raining. When he picked Claire up at her aunt's place, James showed her the cameo and her reaction was enthusiastic.

"Oh, it's really lovely, isn't it? My mother will love it. Especially since it was Grandmother's. The story is sad though, don't you agree?"

"Yes, I read your grandmother's diary, all of it, not just the part where she received the cameo. I found it very interesting and yes, also sad. I was very surprised at the ending though; that you're grandmother married Rev. Houghton."

"Yes, you would have been. I had the advantage of knowing the ending beforehand. I loved my grandfather very much. He was a truly good man. He died when I was fairly young."

"Was he at the boy's school for some time?"

"Yes, he taught there until shortly before he died. There wasn't much else he could do. A career in the Church was not open to him after he married. He didn't make much money there, but I think he did enjoy teaching."

"And are you Catholic?"

"Yes. My grandmother did join the Church, so my mother was baptized and raised Catholic. My brother and I both were, too, even though my father was not Catholic ... he didn't really care much about religion. What about you?"

"I'm also a Catholic. We've been Catholic a long way back. In fact, some of my ancestors were hiding priests from Elizabeth I's soldiers in the 16th century."

"Really! We didn't learn an awful lot about priests hiding from the soldiers of Elizabeth I in school! We just heard of Bloody Mary and all the people she had killed."

"Well, it's not something the English would put in a school textbook, is it? St. Edmund Campion is one priest who was killed during that time, but there were others. Of course, Elizabeth did have some reason to fear Catholics; they weren't all that happy about the changes that had been made. Later, of course, during the reign of James I, Guy Fawkes, a Catholic, was caught trying to blow up the parliament. You probably did study that in school."

"Yes, we did learn about the Gunpowder Plot, of course."

"You didn't attend a parochial school?"

"No. The school where my grandfather taught was a boys' school, and there wasn't a similar school for girls nearby, at least one we could afford. My brother went to the school for a time, though."

"I have always thought that it is rather unfair to call Queen Mary "Bloody Mary" when Elizabeth I killed as many people as she did," James observed.

"Her father, Henry VIII, killed his share, too. I suppose that was what kings and queens did, in those days. I wonder if the prejudice against Catholics, which was so evident in my Grandmother's diary, will ever disappear," she said thoughtfully, "It still exists today, although, I suppose, not so much as then."

"Well, most of the time I'm an optimist and that helped me survive. I think it will get better, and Christians will eventually accept each other. After all, Jesus prayed that we would. If we listened to one another more, there are many things we agree about. But there will always be opposition to the Church from outside; it is, after all, the struggle of good and evil that started in Eden."

They decided to stop for a cup of tea on the way. It wasn't really that much farther to Claire's mother's place, but they had the whole day free. As they entered the cafe, the radio was blaring with Vera Lynn singing, "*There'll be bluebirds over the white cliffs of Dover, someday for you and me.*"

"Strange that they still play that song. We heard it constantly before the end of the war," Claire remarked.

"Maybe they play it because people are still celebrating victory."

Claire nodded in agreement. "Yes, I suppose you're right."

They finished their tea and drove on through Oxford with Matthew Arnold's "dreamy spires" against the afternoon sky. Then they turned north driving through gently wooded country; every once in a while the languid Cherwell River came into view. Soon after, they left the main road, and Claire directed him to a quiet lane. She had him stop in front of a quaint cottage with a thatched roof; a place out of someone's fairytale. A few faded pink roses were still blooming in the front. So this had been Claire Bromley's home as a child!

A small, cheerful looking woman with short, grey hair came to the door and waved to them. Claire introduced James to her mother, and they followed her indoors to the small sitting room. It was much like Claire's aunt's place; a fireplace, a couch, a wireless and a bookcase. On the bookcase there were a few photos. He noticed one in particular; a young man in an RAF uniform. Claire's brother, he supposed. At the other end of the room, there was an old upright piano. The home was cozy but simple. James asked about the history of the cottage, and they chatted a while about the garden and the pleasant weather.

"We have a surprise for you, Mother. At least Captain Marsh does."

"I now live at your mother's childhood home, Markham House," James explained, "When it was being cleaned shortly after I moved in, a brooch was found." James took the brooch out of the box he was carrying and handed it to Claire's mother.

"It's the brooch that Grandmother was given in Italy," Claire added, turning to her mother.

"Do you mean the gift from the Italian tutor?" she asked in genuine surprise.

"Yes, the brooch from Mr. Bartoli that Grandmother mentions in her diary."

Mrs. Bromley took the brooch carefully and looked at it, "Why, it's absolutely lovely," she said simply, "I can't believe this has been found after all these years. Thank you so much for returning it to us. But there must be more to the story. How did you discover it belonged to us?"

Together, James and Claire told the story of the advert he had placed in the paper and how Claire had written to James saying she thought the brooch might be her grandmother's. They filled her in on all the details; James told of Mr. Winston's claim on the brooch and James' suggestion of finding the real owner.

"After Mother died and I read the diary, I wondered where this brooch was and why Mother hadn't kept it if she had cared so much for this Mr. Bartoli," Mrs. Bromley commented, "She must have hidden it and forgotten where."

Claire went out to her mother's tiny kitchen to prepare lunch. They celebrated the return of the cameo with cups of tea, ham sandwiches and strawberries and cream for their sweet.

James asked if Mrs. Bromley had a picture of her mother.

"Yes, I do." And she went into her bedroom to get the photo. It was a photo of Mr. and Mrs. Houghton. They looked almost the way he had imagined them. Claire Houghton was still pretty in the photo, with dark hair and beautiful eyes. She was wearing a fashionable suit and appeared to be very happy. Rev. Houghton looked as he had been described in the diary; tall and thin with a warm smile.

"You look like your grandmother," he said to Claire.

"Yes, people say I look more like my grandmother than my mother."

"And Rev. Houghton looks younger than I would have thought," James added.

"When my Mother first met my father, she was just 18, and she thought he was very old," Mrs. Bromley laughed, "Actually, he was only 39. My Mother used to say, the older she got the younger my father became! He died in 1936 when he was 77 and my mother died three years ago in 1942. She was only 62."

"What a pity the brooch wasn't found before she died," James commented.

"Well, everyone was too busy fighting a war to think about cameos, I expect," Mrs. Bromley sighed.

"And did your Uncle George marry Miss Trent? It was hinted at in the diary."

"No, unfortunately, he didn't. He married a woman who left him for another man. He would have been much better off with Miss Trent."

"Yes, she sounded rather nicer than that." James was sorry he had asked.

"I believe Miss Trent never married," Mrs. Bromley added thoughtfully, "She came to visit Mother a few times, but I was very young so I don't remember her all that well. I do remember thinking she was very beautiful, though."

"And whatever happened to Mr. and Mrs. Fillmore? Did they go to China?"

"Oh, yes. They were there about three years, and then poor Dorothea died ... she wanted a child, but she was older and life was difficult there. I think Mr. Fillmore married again and did have children with his second wife, also in China. I never heard what became of them. We didn't keep in touch. We didn't know him that well, and he wasn't too fond of Catholics, as I recall."

After an enjoyable afternoon, James and Claire left for the trip back home. They chatted about many things on the way; their childhoods, the war, Claire's grandmother and grandfather.

"I said that you look very much like your grandmother, but you aren't at all like her, are you?" James asked.

"I suppose in some ways I am. But I think that nowadays women are much different, generally, than they were in the Victorian era, from what I've read in books."

"How do you mean?"

"Well, today we have careers and we're more independent than they were then. Just think of the women who have kept this country running while you men were away fighting for it."

"Yes, I see what you mean," James agreed, "Do you take after your grandfather more than your grandmother then?"

"I expect there is a bit of both," Claire changed the subject from herself, "Did your faith help you while you were in the prison camp? Or did it make you wonder if there was a God at all?"

"Before the war I wasn't what you would call particularly "religious". When I was at the university, it wasn't fashionable. After, when I was in the army, I wanted to fit in. Oh, I went to Mass every Sunday, that was the way I had been brought up, but I took everything we were taught for granted. While I was in the camp, I had a lot of time to think. Was it all a fairytale or is faith in God reasonable? I decided in the end that it is reasonable. Why had the martyrs willingly gone to their death? Would they die for something that they did not believe in? It doesn't prove that there is a God, of course, but I realized that they wouldn't have died for something that hadn't made a remarkable difference in their lives. I thought a lot about dying then, you see," he smiled, rather grimly, "I even started to pray the prayers I remembered from childhood ... the Rosary especially. I think this gave me hope that I would survive."

Lorraine Shelstad

"I love to pray the Rosary, too. My Grandmother taught it to me. The questions about Our Lady that she struggled with at first eventually led to a deep devotion to her."

"I wondered about that. I want to read more of what St. Thomas Aquinas wrote about 'faith and reason' someday. I think our faith should not be "blind" but perfectly reasonable."

"Someday I'd like to read some of the writings of the Church Fathers, but right now I find it difficult to find the time. We have Grandfather's library and there are so many books that look fascinating."

How wonderful to find someone who likes to discuss the same things I do, James thought.

Chapter 16

After that day, it seemed natural for James and Claire to see each other often. Sometimes they went to see an American movie, usually a Western.

"You can always tell who the bad guys are in an American Western," they would laugh.

Claire never asked about his life in the POW camp unless James brought it up. Occasionally, he would be reminded of an incident and mention it to her but most of the time, like many soldiers, he avoided talking about his war experiences. When he did mention something, she listened, but not with a false sense of shock or horror. She was, after all, used to hearing such stories from her patients.

Just before Christmas, Elizabeth announced that she was engaged. Someone in the House of Lords, no less. James' mother said, rather pointedly, that she couldn't be expected to wait forever. James understood her meaning. Shortly after, he took Claire to meet his parents, and although they welcomed her, he thought his mother, at least, was sorry he wasn't marrying Elizabeth, her best friend's daughter.

James would often collect Claire after her shift at the hospital and drive her back home. If it was a Sunday they would go to Mass together. Other days, they would stop for a drink or dinner, depending on the time of day. On Claire's

Lorraine Shelstad

days off, if the weather was fair, they might go on a picnic; *a merenda*, they would call it, remembering the *merenda* in the diary. They even went punting on the Cherwell a few times.

Once on a beautiful spring day, he was waiting in the hospital garden for Claire to finish her shift. It was almost a year since they had first met. Grey branches were just budding in pale greens, and some bright yellow daffodils were bravely blooming in the flower beds. The cherry trees were bursting into pink blossoms.

From where he sat, James could see Claire in her white, stiffly-starched uniform, helping a young soldier with one leg walk back to the hospital verandah. They were enjoying a shared joke. Claire was an expert at taking the sting out of the tragic. He wondered how he could have ever thought she was ordinary looking! Now, he felt he had never known anyone more beautiful.

As he watched her, it occurred to him that there was really no reason they should not marry. After all, he realized he did love her, and furthermore he didn't want to spend the rest of his life without her. He thought that she also enjoyed being with him. Whether she loved him, and would consent to be his wife, was another thing.

From that time on, he could think of little else except how he would ask her to marry him. He looked for a ring that would suit her small hand and finally found an opal surrounded with diamonds. It was not a large stone, but a large one would not be right for her, of that he was certain.

The day he had planned for had finally arrived. She was waiting for him outside the large, front doors of the hospital. It was a gloomy spring day; wet and chilly. Claire had changed out of her uniform and was wearing a cheerful red dress and a navy Macintosh. Her dark hair had been tied back carelessly, and she looked rather tired from having worked a long shift. When James pulled up, she quickly got in the car to escape the drizzle. He caught the light scent of carnations as she kissed him.

He drove to their favorite pub; a small neighborhood place that felt even cozier and warmer than usual after the wet evening outside.

They found a table near the back and ordered. James' face became serious.

"I've been thinking ...," he began.

"That could be dangerous," she said, laughing.

"Seriously. I've been thinking of buying Markham House."

"Really? Do you think that you'll be posted permanently in England, then?" she asked.

"Well, I don't think so, but I'm not certain yet. In any case, I'll need a place to come back to eventually. I can keep my things there and come back for holidays occasionally."

"That sounds sensible, I suppose."

"I was wondering if you'd like to live there."

"Do you mean look after Markham House when you are away?" She seemed surprised.

"No, look after it when I'm there," he paused, "Actually, I was wondering if you'd marry me."

She looked quite speechless, and James was suddenly afraid she would say, "What a ridiculous idea!"

"Are you saying that you love me?" she asked.

"You know I do," he answered his voice catching. He thought she would have realized that.

"You don't have to tell me right now. You can take time to think it over."

"I don't need time to think it over, James. Of course, I'll marry you. I have loved you since we first met."

James reached for her hand and squeezed it.

He took the small box from his jacket pocket and opened it to show her the ring.

"If this ring doesn't suit you, I can exchange it for something else."

"It's beautiful, James. I do like it ... especially because you chose it." Miraculously, it fit perfectly.

The evening went by quickly as they planned and talked about the future. It was likely that he would be sent to Singapore again as British troops would be stationed there, at least until the new government was established.

"Lee Kwan Yu is a very capable leader. He'll have the country on its feet in no time, but there's trouble brewing in Malaya, and the British need to maintain a presence in Asia."

Claire said she would be happy to live in Singapore and wouldn't mind leaving her work here, "I'm sure I can get work at a hospital there; I expect they always need help."

A few more visits with James' parents and they came to appreciate Claire, not only for how she had helped their son forget a little about his war experiences, but also for herself.

"She's such a dear," his mother once commented.

Several months after their engagement, James heard that he was indeed to return to Singapore. That September, when the leaves were just beginning to turn red and gold, and the weather was still pleasant, James and Claire were married at the small parish church near Markham House. A number of relatives and friends of both families gathered in the garden for a reception after the ceremony. Claire was radiant in an ivory satin gown with lace at the neckline. At her throat she wore a pale pink and cream cameo of the Virgin Mary, a gift from the mother-of-the bride.

Epilogue

Finally, they were on that trip they had promised themselves for so long! James and Claire would see those places that Claire's grandmother had described in her diary ... that diary that had brought them together fifteen years ago. They had returned from Singapore a short while ago. The children were settled in their schools and would stay with Claire's mother at Markham House while they were away. It would be like a second honeymoon!

They flew to Rome first, where Claire's grandmother had never gone. Still, they both wanted to see St. Peter's Basilica, the Vatican museum with its priceless art and the Sistine Chapel. Although preparations were beginning for Vatican II, the historic meeting of the world's bishops from 1962 to 1965, they were still able to see most of the sacred places including the churches of St. Mary Maggiore and St. John Lateran.

The Coliseum was also on their list of things to see and they marvelled at its construction. Then they threw some coins into the Trevi Fountain with the other tourists, hoping to return someday. And they saw the monument to Vittorio Emmanuele II, the monument Italians call the "wedding cake" because it is so ornate and not that tasteful! In fact, they saw everything that tourists usually see and thought everything was superb. James took lots of slides to show everyone when they got back to England.

The trip really began, however, when they took a train north to Tuscany. From the station at Chiusi, they caught a bus and remembered Claire Ashford's description of the "city on a hill" as they approached the hill-town of Montepulciano.

The small *albergo* where they had booked their stay was at the far end of the town. Because buses were not allowed beyond the *Porto al Prato*, they were both exhausted by the time they had struggled up the steep street with their cases. It was probably much the same as the one described by Claire Ashford, but it was not called *Albergo Vittorio* and was not owned by an Englishman. Everything in it was clean, including the rug. The view below was the same as the one Claire's grandmother had described so long ago, with fields stretching far into the distance like a patched quilt of many shades of green. Each evening they saw a spectacular sunset and each morning they heard the bells of the *Basilica of the Madonna of St. Bagio,* just as they had rung over sixty years ago. One day, they walked down the country road to see it; past the vineyards, past the roads leading to farms. When they went in to the Basilica, no one else was there. Their footsteps echoed as they walked on the marble floors and the rays of sun poured through the dome, as they had done so many years before.

Their next stop was the *piazza* and the *Duomo;* the front was still unfinished. Since it was Sunday, they attended Mass where Claire Ashford had been to her first Mass.

The *piazza* probably had more shops around it now. After Mass, they sat at a table in the sun and ordered *lattes,* promising themselves that one day they would have *limonate* in memory of Raffaele.

Of course, they also went to see *Chiesa S. Agnese* and they were told the front had been restored in 1926 but the lovely mosaic of St. Agnes was still above the doors and the beautiful *Virgin of the Milk* was still behind the altar.

The Church of St. Augustine was the same with its wide steps at the front and the statue of Mary of the Assumption with a crown of twelve stars. Claire could see why her Grandmother would have liked it the best.

And of course, *Il Pucinella* on top of the tower across from the Church of St. Augustine still struck the bell every hour to announce the time.

The owner of the guesthouse, Francesca Romana, promised to make arrangements for them to visit the family of Raffaele Bartoli. It seemed that Raffaele's brother had been killed in the First World War, fighting on the Austrian border, but his son, Antonio, now ran the olive estate.

When they made the trip to the farm, Antonio Bartoli met them at the gate. He was tall and slim with a handsome, tanned face and charming manner.

"Welcome to our farm; welcome to Toscana," he said in almost-perfect English, "Francesca told me that your Grandmother knew my uncle, Raffaele."

"Yes, he was my grandmother's tutor when she visited here about sixty years ago. They were very good friends."

"I see. I never knew him, as he died before I was born. Of course, I've heard a lot about him, from my father and from my aunt and of course, my grandparents. He was a great man. Were you told how he died?"

"Yes, my grandmother was told. It was very sad. My grandmother thought he was a good person, too." Claire and James thought it best not to mention the romantic connection between Raffaele and Claire in case it was not known.

Anna, Raffaele's sister, had married and she and her husband had immigrated to Toronto, Canada. Although the olive farm was smaller now, as some land had been sold, the business was actually much larger. Now, they exported olive oil to the United States and Canada and Anna and her husband had been in charge of the business on the Canadian side. Their sons had taken over that business which was apparently doing very well. Claire was disappointed that she wasn't able to meet Anna. She was almost 80 now and hadn't been back to Italy for some time.

Antonio introduced Claire and James to his wife, Susanna, who had prepared a superb Italian lunch of pro-sciutto, fresh bread, fresh tomatoes, cheese and of course, olives. They had some of the local wine with it. It sounded much like the meal that Raffaele's mother had given her English guests years ago.

After a pleasant afternoon they returned to Montepulciano, happy to have met some of Raffaele's family.

The next day they went to Siena and visited *San Domenica*, the Dominican church where they were still able to see St. Catherine's skull. They also visited her home, *Casa di Santa Caterina*, a short distance from the church. Here they saw murals of St. Catherine's life. As Claire's grandmother had not mentioned visiting this place, they concluded that St. Catherine's home was not open to the public then.

Their next visit was to Assisi, in the province of Umbria, where they saw the Basilica of St. Francis and also that of St. Clare. Claire remembered that her grandmother had said the ceiling was very beautiful and she agreed. They still saw many Franciscans in dark brown robes hurrying down the streets. And Claire bought a Franciscan cross in one of the many shops selling religious articles; the kind that Claire Ashford had wanted to buy but dared not because of what the others would think.

The last place they went to was Milan where Raffaele had been killed, even though Claire Ashford had never gone there. They saw the *Galleria*, now with very exclusive shops, and decided they could not afford to buy anything there. They settled for lunch in one of the cafés and watched the *Milanesi* shopping.

Next, they went to the refectory of the Dominican convent and saw the painting of *The Last Supper* by Leonardo da Vinci, the painting that Raffaele had described so well to Claire in his letter. The guide explained that during the war sand bags had been piled up to protect the wall with the famous painting, but even so, it was considered a miracle that the wall had not been damaged, as the rest of the refectory was destroyed by the bombing.

They also saw Milan's magnificent baroque *Duomo* with *La Madonnina* on top; still welcoming people to Milan. Now the city was a busy centre of Italian business and the fashion industry and was very different that it had been during the time of Raffaele and Claire.

Finally, their time in Italy over. They flew back to London from Milan's Malpensa airport. Their memories were full of all the sights, tastes and sounds of Italy. And most of all they were happy to have seen so many of the places in Claire Ashford's diary. The story of the cameo was now complete.

Made in the USA
Charleston, SC
23 October 2011